About the Author

Clifford Chukwuka Okoh was born in Ekuku-Agbor, Nigeria in 1966. He studied Performing Arts in the University of Ilorin, Nigeria and Creative Writing in Birkbeck University of London. He presently lives in London, United Kingdom.

Light in a Trance

Clifford Chukwuka Okoh

Light in a Trance

Olympia Publishers
London

www.olympiapublishers.com
OLYMPIA PAPERBACK EDITION

A CIP catalogue record for this title is
available from the British Library.

ISBN: 978-1-80074-182-9

This is a work of fiction.
Names, characters, places and incidents originate from the writer's
imagination. Any resemblance to actual persons, living or dead, is
purely coincidental.

First Published in 2022

Olympia Publishers
Tallis House
2 Tallis Street
London
EC4Y 0AB

Printed in Great Britain

Dedication

Rita Ngozi Okoh… the light you brought still shines.

Acknowledgements

Firstly, I want to thank my heavenly Father who has made this possible.

My gratitude to everyone who has been a part of this project directly or indirectly. A big thank you to my dear wife, Funmi Okoh, for the unflinching support throughout the cause of this idea, Joshua and Faith for constantly reminding me to write.

Thank you, Janice Okoh, for the encouragement and expert advice on literary matters. My appreciation also goes to the entire Lawrence and Florence Okoh family, to the third generation.

Thank you Kayode and Mayode Ajibade. Thank you, Jonathan Kemp. There is surely light at the end of the tunnel.

As a child in the village, Nkemcho loved listening to bedtime stories often told by his mother. He was so fascinated with the way things functioned in the ancient world of reality mixed with fantasy; for instance, how animals got married to humans and how spirits from other worlds visited the earth in flying banana leaves, that he always looked forward to every evening for a fresh dose. Whenever he thought about these things, a queer smile always filtered across his lips with obvious explanation. He would wonder which animal was going to get entangled with another princess and so forth. Sometimes he found it very difficult to concentrate on school work because his mind was always preoccupied with these extraordinary tales. The thought of what was to come next got him itching to fast-forward the day's activities in order to edge closer to the evening spectacle anchored by none other than his creative mother — the storyteller. His friends at school were tired of him relating these fantastic tales. Although most of them do listen to similar tales, for Nkemcho, his obsession with the storytelling act was incomparable to that of any one of them.

"I can't wait for today's tale. My mother said it will be a blockbuster."

"Nkemcho, you are so carried away with these stories. Why?" Ozo was one of the closest boys to Nkemcho. They lived a stone's throw from each other.

"I love the freedom in these stories and also the extremities. Anything can happen," he chuckled.

"I don't mind them, but I'm not obsessed with them. Of course, I know that it is a form of entertainment. The reality still remains that they are mythologies. Not really true stories, you know."

"I get so sucked in that I feel like I am part of the action.

Sometimes I wish I witnessed some of the very incredible moments of the past."

"Boy, I suggest you concentrate on your studies and forge ahead instead of edging backwards. The future is loaded with goodies."

"I know, Ozo. But you don't understand." They argued on like this until they got home after school.

The moment Nkemcho dropped his bag, the next things on his agenda were food, playing around the compound's near bushes, throwing stones at lizards and low-flying birds. The big moment for him was the long wait for the evening story time. Even though it felt like forever, he did not mind for it was sure that the hour was finally going to come.

Her mother was a fantastic and creative story teller — a tireless narrator. She acted out almost every single sequence of events and played all the characters involved. This she did perfectly by differentiating the voices of the respective characters in the narrative. Easily, she changed her voice to a shivering, yet steady, falsetto, whenever the tortoise was running a scene, and a croaky loud tone whenever the frog took the floor. She always encouraged the kids to try and keep awake so that they could savour the actions and lessons the stories were intended to create. One evening, Nkemcho, who was always awake till the end of every story, drifted off to sleep. His mother did not realise that her son was deep in slumber until the story ended. When all the other kids had dispersed and returned to their respective houses, she tried to wake her son but he was so deep in sleep. This was quite unusual because the boy was not a deep sleeper. She alerted her husband who rushed to the scene. They tried to wake him by pouring very cold water on his body but he slept still. They began to panic.

"But the boy is still breathing," said the dad as he lowered his right ear to Nkemcho's chest. A stream of cold sweat trickled down his forehead. Nkemcho's mother paced around the room more confused than ever. Her wrapper dropped off her chest several times as she went through this unexpected scenario.

"What are we going to do now?" asked the nervous woman.

"As long as he is still breathing, we can just keep an eye on him. It's very late to take him anywhere and I don't want to raise any alarms yet." So, they kept watch. Seconds ticked into minutes and minutes crawled into hours. The vigil lasted until the next morning. The situation remained the same. When it was seven o'clock; the time that the child normally would have been up preparing for school, it dawned on them that something was terribly wrong. They tried the therapy of pouring cold water on him again but it did not change a thing. The boy remained unconscious. His mother knelt down beside him and screamed his name several times. Then she shook him violently but it amounted to nothing.

"We need to get the native doctor." Her husband looked at her directly in the eyes and gave a nod. He could not have agreed more. Nkemcho's mother quickly left the house in search of the village herbalist. After his wife had raced out of the compound, Nkemcho's father drifted into a pensive mood. His eyes seemed like an electronic device that was designed to flick the pages of one's life through time. The unassuming mind of an innocent child would have detected that there was something going on in his inner man. In those days, people tended to wonder who they had offended to merit such punishment. The man's body language was more like taking responsibility for whatever was happening to his son. There was this air of guilt that tormented him greatly.

The chief native doctor arrived earlier than expected. Nkemcho's mother had met him on his way to the farm where he fetched most of the herbs used to prepare various concoctions for his patients. As soon as he stepped into the compound, he was ushered into the room where the boy lay. Nkemcho's mother followed closely behind, stood at his back, and peeped fearfully, as he stared at the motionless body of her son. Slowly he knelt beside the boy and uttered some inaudible incantations. Then he placed his thick palm over the boy's forehead and mumbled some words in quick succession. He reached for his bag and brought out a neatly folded white paper. It looked like a love note. He unfolded it gently to reveal some powdery substance. Then he took a pinch and rubbed it on the boy's face, particularly the areas that surrounded his eyes. He performed a series of spiritual manoeuvres and chanted loads of incantation, and called out the boy's name several times in a bid to wake him up. It failed to yield the expected results. At the end of all the spiritual invocations and traditional abracadabra, he told the parents not to be afraid. The confidence in his look was a great assurance that something good was in the offing. Nkemcho's father felt a bit relieved because for them, the voice of the herbalist communicated the mind of the gods.

"The boy is in the spirit world," he announced. "The worst is that he could be in this state for several days. If he doesn't wake up on the fourteenth day, then that could be a cause for concern."

"What if he doesn't wake up after fourteen days?" asked

the boy's father.

"Then consider him gone."

It was a soft utterance but the effect was devastating for the boy's parents. Nkemcho's mother gave out a loud scream.

"The gods forbid!"

"Control yourself, woman. He will not die." Nkemcho's father had so much faith in the gods. His father schooled him about trusting the watchers of the earth. According to him, they were capable of anything and their nature was kindness and love. He grew up with this belief and practiced this faith doctrine to the letter. He was also told that there was nothing that these gods were not aware of. It meant that handing matters to them at crucial moments was an extreme demonstration of wisdom. Even if fear did creep into his being sometimes, he tried very much not to show it. He looked assuredly to his wife, with eyes that preached peace and wellbeing.

"I'm so scared, my lord." The woman was shivering like a banana leaf under the spell of the rain.

"He'll be fine, my dear."

"Please do not panic. Just keep an eye on him and report any changes as soon as possible. I must be on my way now." The herbalist turned and started to walk away.

"Thank you, wise one," said Nkemcho's father.

The native doctor left. The woman closed in and tucked herself under her husband's armpit. He put his hand round her and clung to her. They stood and stared at each other. One had a feeling of imminent doom whereas for the other, all hope was not lost.

"Let's do as he said. I'm sure if it was a bad situation, he would have let us know." The boy's father assured the mother.

"It's all right, my lord. The gods will never put us to shame."

"You go and carry on with the house chores. I will watch over him for a while." The woman left the room very dejected.

One week passed. It was same story. It became a race against time because according to the spiritualist, fourteen days was the maximum for anyone to be in such a state. They watched the boy for an additional seven days but the situation did not change. The father sent for the native doctor again. He arrived in no time. Then he repeated the rituals, this time pouring a concoction made of fresh leaves and alligator pepper on the boy's body. They waited. The wait was the longest test of patience that they had to go through in a very long time. The native doctor sat down on the floor and brought out a small poche. Inside the poche were seven off-white-coloured cowries. He poured then dramatically on the ground and started to move them in different formations. As he placed the cowries one after the other at different angles, he spoke some words that appeared coded. The expression on his face changed at every point in time. Sometimes, he looked sad, sometimes it was of shock and other times a short smile would appear at the corner of his mouth. All this time, the parents of the boy observed him with maximum concentration. Every moment that passed meant a matter of life and death. Then the native doctor turned and looked up to the boy's parents. The picture that emanated from his pupils was not of a good colour. He began to shake his head as he got up. It was not good news and the boy's parents could tell.

"Now, it's up to the gods to decide. I've done my bit." The herbalist was blunt.

Nkemcho's mother burst into tears. He quickly packed his

stuff back into the bag and made a move to leave. The woman rushed to his side and grabbed him by the leg.

"Please, wise one. You must help us."

"The gods will decide. I must leave now."

***

Nkemcho's father left the house and hurried down a bush path. It was lonely at this time of the day. He whistled a tune and smiled generously. His body language had been transformed into a much more positive one. This produced a euphoric atmosphere that was quite noticeable. The return of Nkemcho from the land of the spirits gave him an overdose of joy. It was undoubtable that his heart was filled up with gratitude to whatever power had brought his son back to life. He greeted everyone that he encountered on the way. There was no telling the difference between friends and foes at this particular moment. A tall woman dashed into the way from the bush. She walked towards Nkemcho's father, clutching an aluminium basin in her left armpit. Their part crossed at a junction that led to another part of the village.

"Good evening, my lord," greeted the woman.

"Good evening, Obias. How are you and the children?"

"We're fine, thanks. And yours?"

"They are doing well. I saw Amara the other day. She's growing to become the next village queen." They laughed.

"Children… I'm grateful to the gods, my dear. Nkemcho almost killed us."

"So, I heard. How's he doing now?"

"He has woken up. It happened a few minutes ago. I call it the miracle of the century. I'm rushing to take the news to the elders forum."

"Thank God. I'm happy for you."

"Thank you so much. I won't be long. Where can we meet later in the evening?"

"Ha! I'm not too sure. My husband won't be hunting tonight."

"Hmm… I wanted us to talk about some important things."

"I really don't know. He's become so suspicious of my movements lately. He almost caught us the last time, remember?"

"We must be very careful."

"I'm not too sure if someone has not whispered something into his ears lately. I sense in my spirit that he's up to something."

"We've been together for so many years now. My love for you is still blazing like a bush fire." He looked around to make sure that no one was eavesdropping.

"I feel the same way too but now I'm married to another. I wish you were the man. I'm getting old with six children down the line. What else do you want? I need to leave now before someone sees us like this."

"Meet me at the usual place tomorrow night then."

"I will try. If you don't see me in time, just know he's around. Goodbye."

Amara's mother, Obias was from the village of Ikwere, a long-time rival of the Owu people. She knew Nkemcho's father and his friend when they used to cultivate a huge expanse of farmland in the boundary between the two villages. Nkemcho's father and his bosom friend made a lot of acquaintances as a result of this and always encountered people from Ikwere village; especially the women who travelled between the farms and the village stream. The two young men teased the young women often and this led to some kind of mutual friendship between them. Obias became very friendly with Nkemcho's father probably because he was the most handsome of the two men. They started a relationship that soon blossomed into a love affair. They remained together until a major conflict erupted that separated the people of the two villages. It was a conflict that left many dead and several others injured. Nkemcho's father lost contact with Obias for seven years because it was forbidden then for them to have a relationship with one another. They were not permitted to cross into each other's territory. When the hostilities between the neighbours died down, Nkemcho's father decided to move to a farm settlement that was on the side of Owu, his village, for security reasons. Life went on and in another two years, he married Nkemcho's mother. Two years later, after Nkemcho's elder brother was born, he ran into Obias in the market square. It was a hot Thursday afternoon. The commercial atmosphere characterised by sounds and voices, both of people and animals, created some kind of organised commotion. Major market activities of the sort only happened once a week. Everyone traded what they had for the things they needed. For other people, using the legal tender was all they could do to pick up important commodities for the week. The environment was a perfect blend of all people of different age groups; the old and young, male and female. Most children who were seen in that environment came to help their parents in the sales processes.

Nkemcho's father tip-toed and hid behind the woman's back. He waited a bit for her to turn her head to the side. He wanted to be close to be sure that she was really the person he thought her to be. The confirmation was positive. It was surely Obias, his heartthrob. His hands shivered as he stretched them out towards her waistline. But midway, he decided on a change of plan. He wanted to tickle her by the waist as they used to do then, but somehow, he was not too sure about the effect that the action would create after many years of involuntary separation. The tap on Obias' back was soft and soothing. The effect was reflective. The young woman jumped around.

"Who's this?"

"Obias. Obias. Is this you?" The smile on his face told a tale of how much he had missed her. The woman jumped on him and hugged him passionately.

"My God. Yekemefuna!"

"Yes, it is me."

"This is unbelievable. I thought I'd never see you again." Obias broke down and sobbed secretly. Some people had noticed the two of them and developed an interest in their conversation. Yekemefuna did not like that so he motioned to Obias by grabbing her hands.

"Come, let's move away from the crowd." They walked within the confines of the market space and found a quiet corner beneath a huge mango tree. They could still see the activities of the people in the market but from a considerable distance. The noise and voices from the market arena filtered into their ears but did not stand in their way of hearing each other loud and clear.

"What are you doing here? This is Owuland." The woman smiled.

"I came to the market to buy some things."

"But you're from Ikwere. Are there no more markets in

Ikwereland?"

Obias laughed.

"I live here now. I'm married to an Owu man."

"It's a lie. That can't be possible."

"But it's the truth."

"Since when?"

"I got married two weeks ago and I just arrived here only yesterday."

"No."

"I'm not lying. It's true."

"Do you know that I'd already started thinking that you had come to spy on us?"

"Really?"

"Yes."

"My husband is from here."

"Wonders shall never cease."

"Yes. He's the man you used to farm with near our village."

"Oh, oh, oh... Tchima?"

"Yes."

"It's a small world. I have not set my eyes on him for more than a year now, ever since he moved towards Umakah village."

"As the saying goes, twenty kids cannot not play for twenty years."

"You're very correct."

"Hope you're doing good."

"I'm very well, thank you."

"And I learnt you got married a couple of years back. How's your wife doing?"."

"Yes. She's doing well too"

"It's a good thing. Nice to see you again."

"Same here, Obias."

"I should be on my way now."

"That's all right. We shall see each other again since you're here now." They laughed.

"Definitely."

"My regards to your husband."

"My regards to your wife too."

They hugged each other briefly and parted ways on that day. For Nkemcho's father, the appearance of Obias in their village meant trouble because he still loved her. Obias on the other hand, saw it from a different perspective. She understood that life sometimes denied one of what they felt they needed most. Even if it was true that she loved Yekemefuna then and now, there was absolutely nothing she could do because it would be wrong of her to have an affair with another man as a married woman. This was not the case with Yekemefuna. His heart had swayed dangerously. It got to a point that he could not sleep at night without fantasizing of how life with this woman would feel. As time went by, his thoughts about Obias grew deeper and began to affect his commitment to his wife.

***

The story about the Owuan people was the big one for Nkemcho. He squatted on the bare floor along with his other siblings and fixed his gaze on his mother. Sometimes, other children from the neighbouring compounds would come to listen to the great accounts of the past as narrated by Nkemcho's mother. The story telling session was always an intense moment. The effect could be seen in the various ways the children reacted to certain aspects of the stories that scared them; especially that of ghosts touching humans and monsters of the evil forest tormenting stubborn children. This story telling ensemble often resulted in half of the children systematically drifting into dreamworld before it came to an end. Nkemcho always struggled to stay awake because he never liked to be either bullied with a knock on the head or stand the risk of missing anything. Some of the kids that drifted into slumber received several knocks from time to time, from the kids like him who managed to stay awake.

Another session was about to start. All the children were seated quietly as they waited for the entrance of the narrator. She stepped into the big room with a lantern in her right hand. Then she sat down and greeted the kids.

"Good evening, children."

"Good evening, ma," they echoed back in unison.

"Are we ready for today's exciting story?" All of them simply nodded.

"That's fine. No sleeping in the middle of the story. Are we agreed?"

"Yes!" The voices rattled in disorganised overlaps.

The woman sat down and adjusted into a certain sitting position that made her look like a bird about to take flight. She cleared her throat and released an enchanting broad smile. The children responded with that shy smile that exposed their innocence and unquestionable loyalty.

"Once upon a time there lived a king…"

***

Owuan village was known in the whole of the east of West

Africa for hunting and magic. The people who lived there migrated from the Nubian peninsula many centuries ago. They were fearless, courageous and highly industrious. The civilisation that existed in that era was created by their forefathers, so it revolved mainly around them. They were more or less the leaders in trade, commerce and craft. They controlled the economic activities of the surrounding kingdoms and villages. This was one of the numerous reasons why other towns and villages around feared them greatly and did everything humanly possible to avoid any sort of confrontations with them. The Owuan people were also warriors who understood the workings and dynamics of nature. They mastered the art of hunting and farming by ancient wisdom that was handed down through many generations. The hunters understood the animal language and behaviours while the farmers by the power of incantations controlled the yielding power of the earth. Their civilisation flourished greatly so it attracted people from far and near.

The kingdom of Owuan had one lineage of kings who started ruling the entire western flank of Africa from the times of the earliest migrants. The kingdom was later expanded to as far as the Congo Basin in central Africa. The people were far from being simple. They were very sophisticated. They had so much respect for their monarch and did everything they could to keep him well and alive on the throne. The king loved his people and represented them well. He particularly enjoyed the way they assisted one another in communal activities. That they had love for each other was unmistakable because they cooperated a lot with each other. They went out of their ways to help their fellow clansmen. There was a practice of old where the entire community came together to give a helping hand whenever anyone was building a house or cultivating a farmland. Every project was community-based and everyone had a hand in almost every good thing that happened in the kingdom. Most of their neighbours envied them for this.

"Children. You must stay awake. I cannot be wasting my saliva for nothing," she said with a big frown.

"Mama, I'm awake." Nkemcho always wanted to be the perfect one among the lot. Some of the kids disliked him for this.

"It's a lie. You were also sleeping," another child challenged him.

"That's enough now. Let's go on." She changed her countenance and jumped back into the character of a storyteller. "We are getting to the most interesting part. One day something incredible took place."

***

The story of man became interesting as a result of the discovery of some artefacts from a village called Zakamapundi, which was an integral part of the ancient Owuanland. The village, famous for fishing, stood on the western flank near the southern border with present day Angola. It was about three hundred kilometres from Wakandi. Before now, there had been several conflicting stories about the real origin of the Owuan people. Some of the accounts were similar while some were totally different. Then came the discovery of these ancient materials which completed the mystery of the puzzle. A series of tests and scientific dating processes were conducted and it was concluded that these people were the first humans on planet Earth. It was the strangest discovery in the history of humanity because there had been no record of the first humans on Earth before this time. The artefacts included a scroll that contained some ancient writings. The language could not be decoded because it was extinct. The search to unravel the mystery of the Owuan people continued until a researcher, Roy Martins, a famous anthropologist from Belgium, travelled to the Congo Basin and encountered the pygmies.

Roy arrived in the Congo and installed himself in a small town called Wakandi. It was about two hundred miles south of the capital city. The long journey from Europe to the Congo had drained his energy. The airstrip where his plane landed and the small town where he was to put up, were about a hundred kilometres apart. The journey by road to Wakandi tore his entire body into bits and pieces of fatigue. On arrival, he was met by the governor general of the region who happened to be a fellow countryman. They drove down to the house where he was to stay and offloaded his belongings.

"Monsieur, Roy. Here we are finally. This is the house. It has been cleaned and sanitized. Everything you need at least for now are intact and a cook has been included for your convenience." The Governor-General was a perfect gentleman.

"Thank you, sir. I'm highly honoured."

"You're most welcome. And one other thing. A native with the name of Jean-Claude will be attached to your research expedition. He understands the terrain and will be able to take you to wherever you desire to go. He should be with us any moment now."

"That's very kind of you, GG. He loved to abbreviate people's names. "Your hospitality is highly appreciated."

The Governor-General left the house and headed north towards the capital. Later, that evening, Jean-Claude arrived. He introduced himself to Roy and ran through a brief history of the town as he knew it. Jean-Claude was fifty-six years old but looked very petite for his age. He had left the Congo jungle many years ago to work in a small town two hundred miles from the capital. His wife and ten children lived with him in a two-bedroom apartment on the outskirts of town.

"The Governor-General told me a lot about you."

Jean-Claude simply reacted with a broad smile. As the two men sat in the veranda talking, the cook; a middle-aged woman with strong African features appeared from the back of the house. She had a green apron. She appeared very neat and cultured but her face was very unpleasant. Roy took a quick look at her and then turned to Jean-Claude.

"That's Magdalene. She's the cook."

"Good evening, sister. Happy to meet you."

She nodded in response; her hands tucked behind her back. "Sir, I wanted to find out what you would want to eat for dinner."

"Any proposals?" Roy responded in a carefree way.

"I thought of making *Ogederi* with grilled fish and tomato sauce." Roy burst into laughter and Jean-Claude soon joined in. Magdalene was a bit embarrassed. She could not understand the reason for their laughter. Was it the way that the name of the dish sounded, she wondered?

"I'm sorry, Magdalene. That was a bit rude I must admit. What's that delicacy again?"

"Ogederi is unripe plantain cooked with fresh pumpkin leaves, sir."

"Sir, you will love it. It's the best dish in the entire Congo Basin." Jean-Claude added.

"I see. Let's give it a try. You can go now," he said to Magdalene who at that moment was itching to escape from the scene. Roy talked through his mission with Jean-Claude over dinner. He showed him a map of the areas that he intended to cover and the goals that he wanted to accomplish. Jean-Claude pledged to do his best for the success of the mission. At around midnight, he left the house in the company of Magdalene. They walked slowly through the wooden gate and vanished into the dark night. Roy retired to his room and soon slept. The environment was very quiet except for the sounds of hunting owls and crickets which continued unabated throughout the night.

The next day, Magdalene arrived the house very early before Roy woke up. Jean-Claude soon followed suit. She went directly to the back where the sounds of her cleaning activities could be heard clearly by Jean-Claude who sat on the veranda; waiting for his boss to wake up. Roy's silhouette surfaced from behind the curtains as he made his way towards the veranda. Jean-Claude sighted him just in time and sprang to his feet; his hands behind his back. It was a gesticulation that denoted respect.

"Oh, you're here, Jean. That's nice. I like punctuality."

He smiled sheepishly. In that part of the world just like many places, the boss was always right. Roy stood and looked around; happy about the early morning sun. He particularly loved the effect created around the environment as the sun rays penetrated the trees, and leaves that formed a large shield to his apartment. Then he yawned loudly and was just about to sit on the chair in front of Jean-Claude when a voice hit him from behind. It was deep and a bit scary.

"Good morning, sir," greeted Magdalene.

"How are you?"

"I'm very well, sir."

"Thanks for the dinner last night. It was very good."

Magdalene smiled. She was like most women. They were happy whenever their cooking got huge accolades.

"Breakfast, sir?"

"Just a cup of coffee for now will do." Magdalene disappeared into the house again. Roy sat down and beckoned to Jean-Claude to do the same. Then he started to explain the day's routine. The coffee arrived without delay. Jean looked at Magdalene in a funny way. It was clear he would have been happier if the boss had asked for a full breakfast. It was a big privilege to eat from the boss's table. After all, it was the call to duty that opened that door of opportunity to him.

Roy took with him a copy of the scroll which contained the ancient writings. One evening he was going through his belongings when Jean-Claude came in with a message from the Governor-General.

He met Roy Martins going through the copy of the scroll and stood behind him for a few seconds. When Roy looked back, he saw that the pygmy man was smiling. He was a bit confused as to what could be causing the wide grin.

"What's the matter?"

"Message from the provincial governor, sir."

"All right… give me a few seconds to tidy up." Roy Martins carried on with the task before him for a couple of minutes. He was, however, surprised to see his assistant; the pygmy man, still standing behind his back. There was this queer smile on his face still. Roy stood up and turned to him.

"Is anything the matter?"

"No, sir!"

"I expected you to wait outside."

"I'm sorry, sir. It's just that I can read some of the things written in that paper you're holding." There was a sharp reaction from Roy. He looked down at the heap of papers on the floor and turned back to the pigmy man.

"Are you serious?"

"Yes, Master. The language is very old." That was how the break came.

"Come. Sit here Jean-Claude." Roy spread the papers, on which the ancient language had been copied, on the floor and the pygmy man began to read and interpret the contents. Jean-Claude was not fluent in this ancient language. Although he tried the best he could, there were still lots of words that he did not know the meaning of. Roy was only able to complete some of the puzzle by logical conclusion.

"How did you come to know about this language," he asked, hands akimbo.

"My grandfather. I used to hear him speak this language with his friends. I was able to pick up some of it because I was the one who served them drinks and food every time they were relaxing in the evenings after farm work."

"And your grandfather must be dead by now."

"Yes."

"Is there anyone that you know who could help in translating this language?"

"No, sir."

"Well… That's all right. What's the message from the governor about?" Jean-Claude reached for his back pocket and brought out a brown envelope which he handed over to Roy

Martins.

"Is there anything you want me to do, sir?"

"Not exactly. Just wait outside. I'll be with you in a moment."

Roy went into the inner room of the apartment and spent a very long time there. Jean-Claude waited patiently but wondered what the hell the man was doing in there. At some point he became afraid and thought that something was wrong. The primitive people thought white men were gods. He was not sure what effect the information he gave to Roy had created. He could hear his voice like he was talking to someone. But to the best of his knowledge, the man was alone, and since he started working with him, he had never noticed any woman near him. So, who could he be chatting with inside, he wondered? The night fell rapidly. The entire environment became so dark. The only light around the place was the lanterns of individuals who occasionally passed by the white man's apartment on their way home from the farm.

Roy stormed out of the room; his face was red and stressed with drops of sweat dripping down his chin. He had in his hands a pile of the copies of the document containing the ancient language. Jean-Claude jumped to his feet; his bladder almost exploding with an unsolicited urge to urinate.

"Sir! Hope you are okay?"

"I guess. But I need your help and it's very urgent."

"Yes, sir."

"Are you sure there's no other person who can help us in translating this language?" Jean-Claude looked down and up in quick succession, his two hands folded behind his back.

"The only person I know is my grandfather and he's dead long ago."

"There must be…"

"Sir, I can… wait. The only person I remember now, is my father's friend who used to work for one of the old men. But he lives very far from here."

"Where does he live?"

"It's deep in the jungle. A three-day journey by foot."

**

"A three-day journey to get to the deepest part of the jungle where the man lived."

The children sighed deeply; their sleepy eyes still fixed on the narrator. Nkemcho looked around to see if someone had dozed off again. His elder brother, Jude, eyed him and gave him a quick quack with his shoulders. The meaning was unmistakable. He had always warned him to only mind his own business. Then their mother panned her shot around the room and slapped her thighs loudly.

"Maybe we should stop here."

"No!" Most of the kids echoed.

"But I can't be telling this interesting tale to sleepy eyes."

"We will not sleep again, ma." Jude spoke out on behalf of the others. He was very mature as a teenager. Although he was as gentle as a dove, he possessed a leadership quality that was next to none. In school, the teachers adored him because he had this quality of organising both his juniors and classmates to good conduct. He was the football captain and the games prefect at the same time. His mother was so proud of him that she could not hide the fact that he was her favourite child. The others were jealous and always accused their mother of been partial when it came to their family matters.

"Jude, please keep an eye on all of them and make sure that no one sleeps while I'm talking." Jude simply nodded. Nkemcho eyed him; his upper lip curled in disdain.

"The journey to the heart of the jungle took three days…" she continued.

Roy Martins and Jean-Claude packed everything they deemed necessary and set out on an early Monday morning before sunrise. The weather was cold and it looked like it was going to rain. The clouds were heavy grey filled with rain. Jean-Claude led the way because he was familiar with the terrain. The Congo Basin was a wilderness. It was about the most dreaded tropical rain forest in the world. It had a mosaic of rivers, savannas, swamps and forests that were always flooded.

As they progressed into the dark part of the jungle, sounds of different kinds began to filter into the air. Little flying monsters dived back and forth and bit them mercilessly. Roy Martins slapped his face and body so much that they turned reddish in a very short time. The dense vegetation and multiple layers of forest cast a gloomy situation around the two men. Roy looked up to the canopy. It was about thirty metres tall. His eyes landed on a group of monkeys as they hopped from one tree to the other. Then he observed the tall trees that littered the forest surroundings. Jean-Claude turned and saw that Roy had his eyes up.

"That is the great Moabi tree. It's about sixty metres tall."

"Yeah, I see."

"We need to proceed. We must cross the Mbezi River before noon."

"Why before noon?"

"There's the great python that comes out to sunbathe

usually at that time. We need to get over before it comes out; otherwise, we would be trapped for hours and won't be able to cross until it leaves at sundown"

"Hmmm… interesting."

"We must hurry so that we can stop to rest and have some lunch before continuing with the journey."

The Mbenzi River was very narrow and dark. The current was strong and could move any object that got into it. The people who crossed the river usually avoided stepping into it. They had to thread down to the point where it was narrow enough to jump over. Jean-Claude was aware of this so when they got there, he explained to Roy Martins what they had to do.

"Be careful, Sir. You must leap over completely and avoid contact with the water." Jean-Claude moved forward and prepared to lift his little frame over the river. He bent low, and lowered his back until it formed a hunch. Then he stylishly glanced at Roy as if to alert him to the ritual pose. Then he leapt like a grasshopper in a swift movement, and landed on the other side. Roy laughed and clapped.

"That was good."

"Now, your turn, sir."

Roy was a much taller man. He was slim and had a solid frame. Jean-Claude stood at full attention. A loose smile escaped the corner of his mouth as Roy positioned himself to leap over the river. But instead of using the pose and technique suggested by his assistant, he decided to do something a bit different. He began by moving backwards up to fifteen metres. The space was expedient to give him enough speed for the much-needed jump. He looked over to the other side, where Jean-Claude stood and observed his steps. If imagination was potent enough to physically put him on the other side, that would have been more than sensational. Time was over for wishful thinking. Only action was needed to achieve the pending objective. Roy took off, throttled in slow running steps, and increased his speed with every step. He resembled a duck in the preliminary stage of a flight. Jean-Claude watched with excitement. Roy got to the edge of the river and was about to lift off when his right leg slipped. The constantly wet ground had mixed with some red slippery mud. He tried to apply his brakes but instead, staggered forward in the direction of the flowing river. The thought of grabbing a tree trunk close by came too late. He tumbled into the river and the current picked him up and pushed him deep until he disappeared. Jean-Claude screamed and thought of jumping into the river but quickly realised that he was a bad swimmer. He did not know what to do. Then it occurred to him to run down in the direction of the current. He ran and called out to Roy. Although he could not see him, he was sure that the river was taking him further downstream. Then he saw two hands calling out for help from the face of the deep but the current was very powerful. Roy could not hold on to anything tangible. The river bank was littered with fresh and rotten leaves. The air smelt of pleasant rottenness. Jean-Claude looked a little farther and realised that the river became wider. He was very sure that Roy would be lost forever if the current pushed him that far. He ran faster and grabbed a trunk which he hurled into the river. Roy who was a bit of a good swimmer got hold of the tree trunk and manipulated his way to safety. The shirt that he was wearing stuck to his body like plaster on a wall. He sat down and breathed like a horse that had just crossed the finish line in a do or die race.

"That was close."

"I was so scared. You should have used my style. Anyway, thank goodness, you're safe."

"The river didn't look like it could move a fly."

"Many people have lost their lives in this same river. I think there's something mystical about it."

"Superstition. It was just an unfortunate incident. It could have happened to anyone."

"There you go again, sir. You guys don't believe in anything. Anyways… hope you're good to go?"

"I guess so."

As they prepared to leave the area, in the distance the forest and the shrubs began to move violently. The rumble was familiar to Jean-Claude. He looked in the direction of the noise and his eyes popped out. Roy saw the terror in his eyes and moved closer to see what he was looking at. It finally surfaced. It was huge; the size of two palm trees put together.

"What's that?"

"We must run fast, sir. It's the huge python."

The two men took off and ran as fast as they could, crashing into trees and grasses that made up the forest floor. When they saw that they had moved far away from the river, and from the primordial reptile, they stopped to recuperate. It was a close shave with the colossal Congo Basin monster.

"That too was superstition?" said Jean-Claude. It sounded like straight mockery. Roy did not reply but simply looked away. The surroundings of where they had gotten were serene. It was void of human life but filled with both visible and invisible entities.

They had a light lunch of bread and sardines and rested for about an hour. While they took the time off, Roy was busy jotting down his observations and a couple of events that had taken place. It was typical of researchers of this extraction to document every single detail of things as they saw them. Jean-Claude cast occasional stares at him as he wrote down stuff. He could not understand why a man who had almost lost his life in an unassuming small river would still have the appetite to be amused with pen and paper. For him, nature was uniquely for observing but his master's orientation would rather explore and search for things that they did not keep. Roy took a clean gulp of more water from the aluminium bottle. Their supply was running very low. They had drunk more than anticipated due to the excessive heat and dehydration. The content in their water bottles had gone down drastically and needed a refill as soon as possible because they still had a long way to go.

"We can fill our bottles at the next river crossing." Jean-Claude got in the lead again pushing through the shrubs and wild grasses as they progressed deeper into the jungle.

"How far are we from there?"

"Two hours journey."

"That's not too bad."

The start-off this time around was a bit sluggish. The race to escape the huge python completely drained their energy. It was worse for Roy because of the earlier ordeal in the fast-moving current of the Mbenzi River. But he was used to the hazards of the road as a scientist. He had experienced similar ordeals in South America and Thailand. The white folks valued the honour received at the discovery of anything new. It did not matter if they lost their life in the process.

The first night that they spent in the jungle was peaceful. They camped under a huge maobi tree. Jean-Claude made a huge fire that managed to burn throughout the night. It did not rain at all. This was unusual.

"The gods are on our side."

"Which gods?"

"The gods of our ancestors that govern the Congo jungle. It didn't rain throughout the night. That's a sign that they knew we were here."

Roy laughed out loud.

"Why are you laughing, sir?"

"It simply did not rain. That's as a result of the weather situation of the time."

"But the fire burnt throughout the night."

"And that was because it didn't rain."

"No. The gods chased the rains away."

"What gods are you talking about?"

"You don't believe in our gods, I know."

"There are no gods, Jean."

"We have gods."

"If you have gods, then they are very unkind to you, don't you think?"

"How?"

"Come on, let's go. I will explain to you." Jean-Claude looked at Roy. He wondered why the white man's opinion was so different to that of the black man when it came to religious beliefs. His thoughts ran back and forth at Roy's statement of the non-existence of gods. Did the colours really matter? This question ransacked his head. Human beings remained human beings no matter their colour or creed, he pondered. Then he concluded in his mind that his boss must be the most foolish man on earth. How could anyone exercise the thought that gods did not exist? He could never comprehend that idea. Nevertheless, the journey progressed. They edged closer to their destination by virtue of the time already spent in the journey. The second night was strange but the third night was very scary. They could hardly close their eyes. A strange phenomenon occurred in the course of the third night. At about one-thirty in the morning, they began to hear a strange chant that was unmistakably human voices. So, they hid behind the big maobi tree and observed the area. They peeped in the direction of the noise and saw light tongues glowing as it approached. When it came closer to where they were hiding, they saw candle-like lamps in a straight procession without anyone holding them. The lamps were literarily walking by themselves. The procession traversed the entire forest floor until daylight. Roy was so perplexed that he could not pen a scientific explanation to the events of that night.

"What kind of lights was that last night?"

"Oh, it was witches and wizards in a procession. They were going to their meeting place."

"It was... really strange."

Jean laughed.

"Another superstition?"

Roy looked at him with a wink.

"There must be a scientific explanation to that..."

"Sir, you never give up, hun?"

"There's always an answer to every question. You just have to figure it out somehow."

When the morning sun appeared, they quickly hurried out of the area. In the distance, they began to hear human voices. They had arrived in the colony of the pygmies where Jean-Claude was born five decades ago.

"We're about an hour from the first settlement. Ours is the

third settlement. Thank God for journey mercies."

"It's peaceful out here."

"We'll encounter more people from now on."

Roy Martins simply nodded and looked around endlessly. His thoughts were focussed on the reason why they had made the dangerous three-day journey into the heart of the Congo Basin. He also pondered on the reaction of the historical and scientific community by the time he was able to unravel the mystery of the ancient language. He imagined how he was going to be celebrated. The gains of research and exploration was unquantifiable. That soft smile filtered across his lips as they descended the hill into the first settlement of the pygmy nation.

The man they went to see was so old that he could hardly see. He was a very small man. Although the pygmies were naturally small and short people, the old man was much smaller, probably due to the ageing processes. He had shrunk into a child's frame. His face made him look like a snowman because he had a long white beard that complemented his all-white woolly hair. His impaired vision was a major setback. The only way out, Roy thought, was for Jean-Claude to read out the document while the old man gave the interpretation or meaning. After the initial introduction and brief discussion about the mission, the old man became very excited.

"This is the story of our people," he said. His face lightened up like the sunrise from the east. He took the two men into a thatched hut. The compound was large with little mud houses. Women and children criss-crossed the compound and chickens, goats and ducks played around, occasionally straying out into the nearby bushes. Inside the hut was very warm. It smelled of fresh leaves that had been boiled for medicinal purposes. The old man sat in a mat knit with palm fronds and beckoned his visitors to do likewise. Jean-Claude sat first and encouraged Roy to sit with a wave of the hand accompanied with a broad smile. Roy looked around the hut and marvelled how humans were able to live there comfortably. He had visited Africa many times but this was the first time that he had the opportunity to witness real primitive life.

"What can I do for you?" The old man set the ball rolling. Jean-Claude cleared his throat and started off explaining in the local dialect. The old man paid rapt attention and nodded his head most of the time. When Jean-Claude was done explaining, the old man got up and walked through a door covered completely with palm fronds that had been shredded. It served the purpose of a curtain. It was put there to prevent anyone from seeing the inside of the room. He stepped out in no time and sat down again. His hands were clutched together. It was very obvious that he had some things hidden in his palms. Roy did not know what to expect at this moment but Jean-Claude was very calm. The old man then stretched forth his two hands and waited. Jean- Claude looked at Roy who was still in a state of confusion. Then he smiled.

"This is part of our tradition."

"I'm lost. What does this mean?" queried Roy

"You watch me and do as I do." Jean-Claude tapped the old man's right hand slightly and bowed down his head. Then he turned to Roy and urged him to do the same. Roy repeated almost exactly what Jean-Claude had done. The old man burst into laughter. Jean-Claude joined him. Roy who did not have any clue as to what all that meant started to laugh with them. Out in the open, several of the very young kids gathered peeping and jeering at the men. A young woman appeared and screamed at the children. She had been observing their antics for some minutes. She spoke in a strong and harsh language. This made the kids run away very fast, scattering in different directions. The chickens and ducks attempted flying off to safety too.

"You are welcome. Tell the white man that I'm ready to help. Human beings are one no matter the colour of the skin." Jean turned and interpreted to Roy what the old man had said. Roy reached for his bag and opened the locks. He brought out all the documents and spread them on the floor. Then he brought out a long exercise book and a pen. Jean picked up the documents and changed his sitting position; and sat on the old man's righthand side. He picked up the first page and read it slowly. The old man spoke every time he paused and he in turn interpreted while Roy wrote down all the details. They did this for hours. When it was around four o'clock in the afternoon, the old man asked to stop so that they could have lunch. Roy was a bit apprehensive about eating the food. It was understandable. The sight of the boiled yam and green vegetable sauce was strange to him. In his eyes were questions that needed quick answers.

"It's good food, sir. Try it." Jean-Claude encouraged him once more.

Roy managed to eat the food. It was not bad after all. He enjoyed, particularly, the vegetable sauce cooked with fresh fish. After the meal, fresh palm wine was served. They drank until all Roy wanted to do was to stretch out on any flat platform and sleep. Jean-Claude laughed at his master as he staggered to the room that the old man had prepared for them. The end of another eventful day. Jean-Claude was happy to be home again after several years in the city. Later that night, he went back to the old man's room where they resumed drinking and chatting till the early hours of the morning.

The one-hundred-and-fifty-page document took seven days to translate. Roy and his assistant spent an extra day with the old pygmy man and his large family before they returned to town. Roy offered the old man a silver coated lighter before they left that day.

"This will be useful for making quick fire and also to light up tobacco."

"Help me to thank the white man," said the old man. "My friends will be envious of me when they see this." He scrutinized the object and smiled in great satisfaction. Then he prayed for Roy and Jean-Claude and bade them farewell.

They arrived at the sleepy town of Wakandi after another three-day journey through the Congo Basin. Roy tidied up the translated document and went through it before he went to bed on the third day after their arrival. He had asked Jean-Claude to take a break for two days to enable him to have some good rest. He needed uninterrupted time to read through the story and draw an initial conclusion before informing his research partners in Belgium. In the night he drank a black coffee, prepared by Magdalene after dinner and descended on the finished work.

***

Okotoba was one of the most prominent hunters in the kingdom of Owuan. One day, he decided to go hunting alone because two of his mates had declined the offer to go into the forest in search of bush meat. It was a quiet and breezy Sunday evening. The chickens were scrambling to roost while the nocturnal birds with their coded whistling sounds mesmerized the evening atmosphere. The commencement of their nightly activities was about to begin. Okotoba hurried into the main bush path clutching a small bag made of animal skin. He also had a locally manufactured machete and other materials like ropes made from climbing plants, and metal rings used to set traps for medium-sized animals. As he went in the direction of the farm settlements, he came across people, especially women, who were returning back to the villages from their respective farmlands. He exchanged pleasantries with each and every one of them. It was the custom.

He was not the only hunter in the village and its environs who was on a game mission this night. A lot of hunters did hunt in the night and they did so for obvious reasons. For one, some animals only came out in the open to source for food at nights while for others, it was a good time to catch some good night's rest. Both situations favoured night hunting.

Okotoba advanced into the deep forest shortly before midnight. In their dictionary there did not exist any word called 'fear'. As he walked confidently deep into the night, sounds of different animals filtered into the air. It was very familiar. Sometimes, he would whistle back the exact same sound that the animal had made. Some people believed that some animal sounds were not really made by animals but by evil spirits who had the habit of obstructing the hunters' quest for game. So, it was productive to repeat such sounds because the evil spirits interpreted them for greetings from the human beings. As he brushed through the wild grasses, sleeping birds flapped their sleepy wings and flew into the dark night for refuge. Okotoba was not after birds. They did not even qualify for snacking as far as he was concerned. He was in search of the big game — the antelopes, bush pigs, grasscutters and huge pythons. The forest turned darker as he moved further in. The tiny twinkling lights from the sky had now been blocked almost completely by the covering caused by mighty trees that lined the length and breadth of the entire landscape.

In the distance appeared a bright light. It was very tiny but was quite penetrating. It began to flicker without precision. He stopped and observed the strange beam. Then he looked by his side and reached for the bag made of antelope skin which hung across his shoulders. It could be other hunters, he thought. He whistled a code but there was no reply. Usually, hunters communicated with each other in whistling codes to indicate their presence in an area or as a means of identifying other hunters nearby. At other times, they would whistle in very high tones and frequency to attract the attention of hunters who are far away. His left hand went into the bag in a hurry. The phenomenon was nothing he could explain at that point in time. He ransacked the leather bag without really looking into it. By the time his hand was out of the bag, a cone-like object with a red cloth tied around it drilled the dark night. It was the size of an egg and it looked like the shell of a marine mollusc. He slowly started moving on the spot in what appeared to be a dance ritual. He muttered words, melodies and incantations as he moved almost in slow motion. The spotlight in the distance glowed still and grew dimmer. Then it exploded into a big flame, lighting the entire area. Okotoba looked up to the skies and thanked the gods. He realised it was not other hunters but witches on their way to their nocturnal rendezvous. A broad smile on his face was unmistakably a thrill as he continued his journey further into the night.

Owuan woke up the next morning to pandemonium. The village had never witnessed this level of noise, confusion and movement for centuries. It was supposed to be a market day. The women who were early risers had in fact displayed their wares before the break of dawn. The news came in a bit later as the day was breaking with the rising of the sun. No one knew what the situation was. Everyone had a different tale to tell, and people were running back and forth. Some said a strange animal had appeared in the village, killing people while others claim that a hunter had been killed by an animal that was half beast and half human. A lot of people were running to the king's palace for different reasons. Some thought it was a good place to seek refuge while the thinkers and the powerful men thought that the monarch must need some kind of extra security measures around his palace.

The palace was filled with subjects who came to take refuge and soldiers who came to protect the king. The guards mounted a barricade to the inner courts of the king's palace. People waited to get more authentic news. More people had arrived and the entire environment waited patiently. The crowd was so tight that the fear of a stampede occurring became imminent. This would have been catastrophic. After a long while, the noise ceased. All eyes focussed on the entrance to the king's inner chambers. An outward movement of a few guards explained the reason for the sudden silence. The king was coming out to address the people.

The king appeared in his majestic apparel, a few of his top advisers followed closely behind. As the train proceeded to a stage-like platform, clearing up the pathway to the inner chamber, four men appeared. They were carrying a man on what looked like a stretcher made of animal skin. As they came closer, it became apparent who the man was. The man had a human head, his right hand was like that of a crocodile, the left arm like that of a hyaena, his left leg was like a python and the right leg resembled that of a leopard. It was none other than the hunter Okotoba. The entire crowd went cold. Then they began to whisper in low tones. The king took a concentrated gaze across the crowd and cleared his throat.

"It is a sad day in our kingdom today, my people." He paused for a while and looked deep into the crowd. "Our brother, Okotoba has done the abominable and the gods have struck him with a plague. Look at him. Just look at him. He is now half-beast and half-human". The crowd erupted in sympathy for the hunter. The noise died down gradually and everyone bowed down in utter disappointment. It was a gesture of fear and pity all woven into one. Then the king continued. "He has tasted of the forbidden meat in the evil forest. The gods are very angry because he ate the giant *usu*[1]. The gods are very angry, and the consequences are unimaginable. The entire kingdom will witness sickness and disease, and many people will die. As for the porter of this misfortune, he will be taken back to the evil forest where he will face the wrath of the gods in a furnace. Okotoba will be burnt alive. His offspring to the fourteenth generation, shall labour to build the earth as a punishment for this evil act committed by their father. I have spoken."

The crowd made a unified sound that connoted empathy and fear. Then they began to disperse slowly like ants whose edifice had been destroyed by a strong intruder.

---

[1] bat

47

***

"Was he really burnt alive?"

"Nkemcho, you're too forward. I am the story teller. You need to exercise some patience." The other kids agreed by nodding their heads violently.

"The story has not ended yet, children. There's more. In fact, when the king had finished making the pronouncement, the palace poet picked up and started to chant some phrases."

DARKNESS, oh darkness. Why do you cover the face of the light?
See how suddenly, fiction turns to reality overnight
WILD fantasies of age long dreams begin
To break forth like flowers blooming at the yearning of spring

It is the dawn of a panic festival; a dance of uncertainty
In the face of a pandemic
The news spread like a wild fire
Spewing syllables of uncontrollable desires

So, we turn to the powers that be
But all we hear is an assurance of safety unreal
Then come the tale of the DO NOT...
Wielding that draconian school of thought

Do not touch your face
Do not touch your mouth place
Do not touch your nose
Do not even touch your eyes closed

And then the myth of Do's
Announcing the twist of the blues
Do wash your hands regularly
And sanitize on sea, air or land as the case may be

The film has just begun...
People are dropping dead... the healing houses are
overwhelmed with the sick, no bed
This looks like the beginning of the end
Or the end of a glorious beginning my friend
Why is the divine silent?
And the sonorous voices of pharisees and spiritual healers
gone dead?
Technology has put sugar and carbon dioxide in our mouths
Hoping we make a good choice under the dark clouds

Mankind is under siege
Everyone is speaking a different language
Some are too confused to understand what's going on
While others stand and watch catastrophe unfold under the
red sun

It is like a battle of the forces of evil over good
A reality stranger than fiction but true
We have been through this road before, I remember.
We did struggle a lot before we woke UP from our slumber.

The children hurried to their respective rooms as soon as the
story time ended. The other kids had run back to their
compounds as fast as they could because it was already very

late in the night. Nkemcho's mother walked gently across the hut to the bigger hut near the front entrance and disappeared through a small door. The next morning, Nkemcho woke up and saw his father preparing to go out. He was putting some oil in the chain of his shiny silver coloured bicycle when his wife came out from the backyard.

"I thought you had gone to the farm." Nkemcho's father started.

"No. I was preparing the bitter leaf soup at the backyard."

"Oh, I see. That's good. I will eat some when I come back."

"Where are you off to early this morning?"

"The chief of Owu clan asked me to deliver a message to the elders of Ikwere. They've started again. Some of their men were seen encroaching on our lands by the Amanze riverside."

"Why do they like so much trouble, these people?"

"I don't really know."

"And some of their women are married to our men in this village."

"Very true. Amara's mother is from Ikwere."

"Even Nkokiru's mother is from there too."

"I know that. In fact, the two villages used to be one until the white man came and broke it into two. Since then, we have not known peace. They claim that part of their land was partitioned on our side.

"Please take care. They are very wicked people."

"I will, my dear." The man rode off into the dusty road as Nkemcho watched from where he was standing.

"Nkemcho, you will be late for school." The hard-working woman started to walk towards the backyard from where she appeared earlier on. Nkemcho dashed into the room and resurfaced with a wrapper tied across his neck. He quickly picked up a yellow plastic bucket and ran to the back to get some water.

"Don't forget to cover the drum when you're done," the mother screamed behind him.

Nkemcho's father, Yekemefuna rode majestically out of his neighbourhood, saluting people he met on the way. He was well known for his knowledge of farming and also for his expertise in tapping wine from the palm tree. He arrived at a crossroad called three ways. One direction led to Ikwere, the second one to the outskirts of the two villages while the third led back into Owu village. Instead of following the direction of Ikwere village, he turned slightly left to the way that led to the outskirts of the villages. He rode for almost twenty minutes before arriving at a bush path that was very narrow. He stopped and jumped down from the bicycle. Then he observed the quiet environment for a while. He had to use one hand to push back the overlapping leaves that almost covered the pathway and the other hand to direct the bicycle. He continued along the bush path and arrived at a slightly opened space. There was a long bench that had been mounted in front of a small hut. This was the location of his palm wine tapping business. The hut looked quite old but it was very obvious that people frequented the place. Evidence of human activity could be seen everywhere, ranging from wrappers of food to calabash bowls; used for drinking palm wine. Other household utensils were all over the place. Yekemefuna rested the bicycle near the wall of the hut and began to pick up the litter. When he was done, he thrashed them in a heap of rubbish and set fire to them. Then he went into the hut for a few minutes, perhaps to tidy it up. The voices and sounds of people as they passed could be heard clearly. Yekemefuna came out with a loud yawn. Then he looked at the bench and noticed a yellowish stain. It was very dry. A quick investigation confirmed the stain to be waste product from a bird in flight. He heaved a sigh of relief. The rural area was a peaceful place but there were a lot of evil deeds that one could never ignore. Sometimes, some jealous people deposited charms in farms or places of business that belonged to other people. He thought someone had deposited some charm on the bench. He re-positioned the bench after dusting it thoroughly and his attention was drawn to the rustling of the branches that covered the path. A figure soon appeared. It was the beautiful Obias. He ran straight towards her with a broad smile. He held her tight in a warm embrace and lifted her off her feet.

"Put me down."

"You took so long. I was beginning to get worried."

"My husband became a bit suspicious so I had to wait until he went out."

"Where is your bicycle?"

"I left it at the usual place." They walked hand in hand and settled on the bench.

"I'm so glad you made it."

"Do I have any choice?"

"Come, let's go inside. My body is already on the road." They laughed and Yekemefuna dragged her into the hut.

***

Okotoba died shamefully. This was several centuries ago and Africa had become the mother of the entire world with everyone therein. Life did not end there for his lineage because he had a family that transcended many generations. One of his descendants involuntarily left Africa. He was captured in a slave raid. It was the era of the survival of the fittest; a time when people were forcefully transported across the Atlantic to the New World. The white man's influence was all over the face of the Earth. They had jump-started civilisation from where their African ancestors left it. Slaves have been evacuated from their roots and taken to strange lands. Jamoka was one of the many foreign places that these slaves were taken to work in plantations. In this time, sugarcane was the posh commodity of the day as far as farming was concerned. All the blacks on this island were slaves who worked on plantations owned by their white masters.

Mabarika, a young black girl, thirteen years of age, her parents lived and worked on one of the thriving sugarcane plantations owned by one Mr Greene. He was a European merchant and successful businessman. Mabarika was young and beautiful. She had a very dark but shiny skin. A typical African woman, excellent curves, succulent breasts with large nipples that seemed to be pointed at the heavens. Her behind was huge and good to look at any time she walked past. Also, she had shiny white teeth and the most seductive smile. She loved the plantation so much and saw the owner as part of her family. Perhaps she was too naïve and uneducated to really understand what it meant to work in a plantation owned by a white man at the time. She freely moved and played with other black kids in the plantation as if they owned it. Although, she sometimes witnessed workers being subjected to excessive maltreatment, she never saw the situation from a racial perspective. Every aspect of life within the agricultural enclave seemed to be very stable until the famished eyes of the plantation owner found the young lady one Sunday evening. She had this routine of taking dry sugarcane stalks to the barn for the animals to chew on. It was a task that she carried out day in and day out. It was basically part of her duties on the farm. The only strange thing was that Sundays were reserved as rest days by Mr Greene. He was always angry whenever he saw anyone doing any work on Sundays. He understood that the workers needed to recuperate for at least twenty-four hours before jumping back on the beat when the new week began. On this fateful day, he asked Mabarika to take some stalks to the barn. Her parents did not frown at it because they knew that the boss never wanted anyone to work on Sundays. He probably needed to sort out that task before the new week began.

Mabarika was excited to carry out the orders of the plantation owner. His wish had always been their command at any given time. The barn was there as usual. Nothing changed. The horses were grouped into the larger part of it. The cows and goats occupied a smaller part. She brought the first set of stalks and deposited them at the base of the entrance to the place that housed the horses. She brushed past Mr Greene as she was going to get the second set of stalks. Their eyes met but she quickly looked away. He had his hands at his back, face to the ground and a relaxed demeanour. The young girl soon came back and deposited the stalks this time in front of the wooden gate where the goats were kept. As she turned around to go for the third set of stalks, she bumped into the boss who had been standing behind her without her knowledge.

"I'm sorry, sir," she apologised.

"It's all right. Come this way." Mabarika avoided his eyes

all this time. In fact, it was a sign of respect not to look into the eyes of an older person while engaging them in a conversation. She followed him into an inner chamber used by the boss to take stock of the animals from time to time. It was a square room built with heavy logs of wood. The logs were placed on each other so tightly that there was barely an open space to peep into the fields.

As soon as she arrived there, free from view, the boss pounced on her. Mr Greene was like a lion who had cornered its helpless prey. Mabarika was terrified. She had never seen the man in this state. The barn was a bit far from the building where she lived with her parents. He knew that her screams would amount to nothing. The only thought that came racing into her head was that she had been tricked by the boss. The sky up high, and the ground down below was not in any mood to provide some sort of succour for the vulnerable young lady. She had been caged between the thick walls of the barn and her unrepentant aggressor.

Mr Greene pushed her to the wall, tore the light tattered top she had on and grabbed her breasts. Mabarika was so terrified and confused that she could not fight back. He pinched her large titties until it hurt. She was too scared to shout. She groaned in style so as not to provoke the shameless old bully. Then he turned her around in a swift and precise movement, and forcefully pulled down her skirt. He smiled at the view of her massive backside. Then he dropped his trousers. The sexual ordeal was brief. In less than five minutes, he let her off. He warned her never to mention this to anyone. Then he gave her a piece of dirty cloth to clean up the blood that streamed down her thighs. The girl wept inside and felt worthless. She managed to walk back to her house without anyone noticing that something was wrong with her. That night she had a nightmare. She kept screaming out from her sleep. At some point, her mother came and laid down by her side. She perceived that all was not well.

"My dear, is this all a nightmare?"

"I guess so."

"Tell me, I'm your mother. I think that you're keeping something from us."

"Nothing, Mom. I will be fine."

"Just that you will be much relieved if you share it with someone especially your mother." Tears began to drop from her eyes as her mother demonstrated love, care and understanding through her soothing words.

"It's Mr Green." She sobbed. Her mother pulled her very close and caressed her back.

"Did he?"

"Yes, Mother. He forced me."

"Oh my God!"

"There was no one to help me, Mother."

"It's all right, my dear. That's our lot in life. One day we shall overcome." Both mother and child consoled each other and cried till the morning light. Mabarika's mother later told her husband what had transpired between their daughter and Mr Greene. The rage in her husband's eyes spilled fire but he could not confront the rapist. Who was he to question the authority of a man who owned his life? The sense of misery and pain that he felt was unquantifiable. Yet, he could not do a thing.

That was how Trebor Atsen was born by a young slave girl who was taken advantage of by the owner of the plantation where her parents worked. Mr Greene had forced himself on the vulnerable young girl and that was all about it. The matter did not see the light of day. It ended the way it began and there was nothing the parents could do about it. They were ordinary slaves that had no rights. Her mother cried so much but tears were not enough to undo the damage that Mr Greene had done. Her father wished he had the guts. He desired to kill the man and face the consequences. It was a wish of the spirit that the body was too weak to implement. As for Mabarika, it was the biggest and most shameful assault on womanhood. It was an experience that she could not get over. She then entertained a thought to run away from the plantation. She was too ashamed of herself that remaining there, she thought, would have turned her into a laughing stock; especially among the young slave boys who had been making passes at her since she began to advance into puberty. Her parents tried all they could to console her but it amounted to nothing. They could not restrain her either from pursuing her project of eloping into the unknown. Their efforts yielded no results because she had already made up her mind to leave.

Eventually, she escaped with the help of one of the guards who had been her admirer since she was eight. She could not stand the face of the man who turned her life upside down. Her final destination was Pitfalls, a suburb in the capital city. She settled down in no time and began to raise her son as a single parent.

The young Trebor Atsen ran the streets with other kids until they were teenagers. Life for them was more than tough. All of the kids suffered hunger, deprivation and neglect. Trebor Atsen soon noticed that he was different in skin colour so he started asking lots of questions. His mother could not tell him the truth. It got so bad that other kids teased him and made fun of the fact that he was neither white nor black. This upset him so much that he withdrew into himself and started a journey of self-discovery. In the process, he discovered singing. His voice resonated power, justice, freedom for the oppressed. He started to write revolutionary lyrics which he sang to his friends every evening. Word soon spread across the entire neighbourhood of this talented teenager. Other kids started to emulate and imitate his good virtues. The seed that was sown out of greed and violence had become a mustard one. Trebor's influence grew into a big tree where the people came to seek refuge. They dropped down their ears to listen to redemption songs and other revolutionary lyrics. The awakening of their dormant consciousness spat fire like an angry volcano. More people including adults and the elderly started to attend his evening gigs which were held in the open. The rejected stone finally became the corner stone. These ideologies of freedom and equal rights being championed by Trebor Atsen grew so strong amongst the youth that it became a gradual movement. The young and vibrant Trebor soon became the senior advocate of this new school. He later teamed up with two of his friends and formed a band. For them, music was a powerful tool for the fight against injustice. If they did not have money and power, their voices were good enough to match up with that of the oppressors, they thought.

One evening, Trebor escaped from the many souls who came to listen to his revolutionary songs, and headed towards the wilderness in the outskirts of Pitfalls for inspiration and spiritual cleansing. From times of old, the idea of separating oneself from people and human activities for spiritual purposes was very popular. This was particularly common among spiritual heads and prophets who served as links between the people and God. Trebor took only his acoustic guitar. He had the intention of spending three days there all in a fast. No food, water and smoke for three days and three nights was the sacrificial offering in return for spiritual rejuvenation and empowerment.

He settled in a cleared part of the forest. The landscape was uneven because it was a land that had hills and valleys. Trebor positioned himself on top of one of the highest hills from where he could easily savour the beauty of the surrounding natural architecture. In the far distance was the beautiful waters of the Caribbean Sea. The air around this vicinity was usually very sweet. Oftentimes, the area got very busy with bush men who had dreadlocks that ran all the way to their backs. It was a place of high meditation and a safe abode for those who smoked the green leaf. Sometimes, the sound of crying acoustic guitars escaped the valley and struck melodies up the hill. The sounds of weird chants were a regular occurrence in this wilderness of the gods. It was the secret place where divinity interacted with the flesh. Trebor started by singing praises to God and worshipped Him in spirit. His voice was strong and sharp like a two-edged sword designed to cut asunder the shackles of bondage. The praise and worship songs lasted for over twenty minutes. Then he switched to prayer mode and thanked God for his love and goodness towards him and his family. As the cool evening breeze began to whistle tunes into the night, Trebor picked up his guitar and simply strummed some single notes. It appeared as if he was tuning the instrument. He continued to strike different notes and gradually came out with a progression that emanated from the G-major chord. The rhythm of his guitar permeated the environment like the sweet aroma of the green leaves did when the bush men visited the holy place for their occasional pilgrimage. He played and mumbled some lyrics until the call of nature dawned on him. The power of the ever-consistent night visitor hit him and he drifted into slumber afterwards. Day One was a peaceful night.

In the morning, he woke up and repeated the prayer routine before taking a walk down the hill near the river. He spent most of the day downhill in meditation. In the evening, he mounted the hill again and spent the second night quietly. The third night was however different. He slept as usual but was awoken by the rush of violent wind. He struggled to open his eyes but they felt very heavy. The only thing he could do was to turn face down. In this position, he lay on the bare rock. Then a tap on his shoulder sent cold chills down his spine. He could not turn around but heard the voice. It was still, small and had great authority.

"Get away from me. I'm only here to pray."

"You have done well, my son."

"Who are you?" Trebor was terrified.

"I am who you think I am." The voice was very steady.

"What do you want from me?"

"Just to deliver a message. I am a messenger."

"Speak, for my ears are down."

"For deliverance is a need for the captive and love is a picture image of the painter. Everyone was born to fulfil destiny. Yours is in front of you. Never rescind from what you seek. The truth never dies. The age long tale is worth discovering. Go in peace and make the world a better place."

Trebor jerked to consciousness after the last statement. He had been dreaming all this while. He sat up and scrutinised the surroundings once again. He always did that. It had become a ritual. However, the result was good. The area was still very calm and serene. There was nothing to fear after all. The words spoken by the stranger continued to echo in his head. He could feel a slight headache but he appeared to be very well. The remaining hours of the morning were spent thinking about the words of the messenger. He began by assimilating the contents. He tried to decode the meaning but it was not forthcoming. Some instinct told him to just memorise the message and forget about the interpretation until a later time. Deep inside his being, he could still hear the voice talking to him like a constant reminder. When the morning finally came, he picked up his guitar and went down the hill. He dipped his body in the clear river that ran through the wilderness and had a wash that lasted only a couple of minutes. Trebor went back to Pitfalls afterwards, strong and well revived.

The musical group known as Masai was born out of necessity. They choose that name because it symbolised great courage as demonstrated by the fearless Masai people of the Kenyan plains. They were the only people known for the extremely courageous act of stealing kills from the lions and other wild cats of the Serengeti. The musical group, Masai, represented strength, determination, courage and change. Trebor, Johnny and Matty were a bundle of talents. They were songwriters, fantastic singers and multi-instrumentalists. They sang tirelessly, day through night in the neighbourhood, played in local bars and events places till they had a break into the limelight. The group was discovered by Ricky Townsend, a roving European label owner who came to Jamoka on holiday. Time and chance finally found and smiled on them. They became an instant success and toured the world with hits that busted the music charts. It was out of the ordinary for ghetto kids to control the activities in the entertainment scene that had long been dominated by white folks. Trebor who was the leader of the group was also the lead vocalist. He had a powerful and rebellious voice that matched the very ideals of the movement. His music became a weapon, an instrument to suppress oppression and injustice. He became very vocal and spoke with passion and great wisdom. The press always gathered around him like Saharan house-flies on dead animal carcasses in the dry desert landscape. In one of his tours somewhere in the east Pacific, a press conference was organised by the promoters of the show. The concert was a few hours away. Trebor wanted to do the press conference before mounting the stage. He left the hotel with his crew and headed to the venue. All the pressmen and women that were invited had taken strategic positions by the time they arrived.

Trebor Atsen walked into the room where the journalists were already waiting. There was a quick round of laughter in the charged little room because one of the journalists had said, "Here comes the lion." He settled into a chair and smiled, looking excitedly at every face. Trebor was a calm, simple gentleman. He smiled all the time. Four of his band boys later came into the crowded room. They squeezed themselves in a corner and fixed their gaze on the leader of the band. They loved him so much because he was humble to a fault and carried everyone along in the most professional way. They also believed in him because his words were always true and a perfect fit to very crucial moments. The interview soon kicked off.

"Thank you Trebor, for honouring our invitation." The first journalist was from the government owned media organisation called the *Pacific News*.

"I'm most delighted to be here. It's my pleasure." Trebor smiled and caressed his long beard with his right hand.

"The first question I would like to ask you is this… How would you describe your music?"

Trebor gave him a quick smile as usual and withdrew a little bit into himself. His countenance changed almost immediately. Then he sighed deeply, looked at the journalist straight into the eyes and began to chant…

My music…
My music is…
My music is the sounds in my head, the beat of my heart, the tears that I cry — and…
My music…
My music is…
My music is the fart in my ass, the rain from my pipe, the regrets of my past — and

My music is life
My music is riches, not in diamonds and gold and precious stones but courage to be bold, not desiring the power of the throne
My music is the race of humanity
My music is the joy of equality
My music is me in control
Of positive vibes for the body and soul

The press conference lasted for over an hour. At the end, they all proceeded to the venue of the musical concert. The stage was set, all instruments in place and stage lights were beaming colours of every kind. The band climbed the stage and started to check the equipment. Trebor had been there during the late morning to do the sound check with the entire band. The excitement was electric. The band began to play slowly in the background while Trebor stood aside very close to the staircase that led up the platform. After about ten minutes, the master of ceremonies mounted the stage to kick-start the show.

"Ladies and gentlemen… all the way from Jamoka… join me to welcome the one and only Trebor Atsen and the Masai." The audience exploded in excitement. They screamed, shouted and whistled continuously. Trebor mounted the stage and the show began.

The concert lasted for several hours. The level of energy on the part of the musicians and the spectators was unimaginable. The entire arena was electrified when Trebor sang the hit track entitled *"Awake from your slumber."* It was so emotional because almost every mouth echoed that song from the beginning to the end. For Trebor, it was the whole essence of the music — the fact that people get touched by the sound. It was such a great delight. Everyone had a first-hand experience of the punchy and revolutionary effect of the lyrics. The crowd always had this fetish feeling every time that they listened to the songs of Masai. It was the unique pattern that always accompanied the music and it sounded good to the group. Trebor and his band finished the concert in the early hours of the morning. The hotel where they lodged was packed full with fanatical fans who still could not get enough of them and their musical stuff. There were lots of women around the hotel premises. They began to scream and shout as the bus conveying the band made its way into the compound. Trebor simply looked out the window and waved at them. The next day they took a long flight back home.

Trebor drove to the library in company of the band's manager, McRoy. There was a book that he wanted to read. Someone had mentioned that book to him a couple of weeks back. It was not too difficult to find the book because it was a historical account that no one was interested in. They went through the procedures and borrowed the book. In the car, Trebor flickered the pages and could not wait to start reading. He was a busy man who barely had time to do things other than music. But this book had so much that he wanted to learn about. He rolled back the pages again and started this time from the first chapter. He got engrossed after reading the first page. The second chapter took him to the historical account of Okotoba, the great hunter of Owuan kingdom

A couple of centuries after Okotoba was sacrificed to the gods in the evil forest, some of his descendants decided to migrate out of Owuan kingdom. The shame of being part of a lineage that brought misfortune to the entire kingdom became too hard for them to bear. Apart from the fact that people often referred to them as bearers of misfortune, it became the fashion to blame every negative occurrence in the kingdom on the event that took place many hundreds of years ago. The leader of the Okotoba lineage at this time was Makuka. He was a successful craftsman. He made most of the artistic pieces and decoration in the king's palace and designated cultural sites around the kingdom. As a highly talented artist, he thought that his work could have earned him respect strong enough to overshadow the events of the past. The stigma had become so unbearable that he thought the best thing to do to secure the future generation was to move to a far place where no one would judge them by the conduct of their ancestor.

Makuka mobilised the entire Okotoba family lineage and one early morning before the village woke up, they left. They journeyed north-eastwards from where came their ancestors. They crossed kingdoms, and villages, and rivers and forests, and open plains until they arrived very close to the Sahara region of north-eastern Africa. Makuka was a young, vibrant man in his early forties when they left Owuan. By the time they arrived in Egypt, he was eighty years old.

They had not been settled for a year when Makuka called a meeting of all the family members. He narrated to them a dream he had and gave them the instructions handed over to him by the gods.

"This land is not our destination, they told me. We are to occupy the entire land space to the ends of the earth."

"How can that be?", asked Muiz, his eldest son.

"We're going to divide the Okotoba clan into seven groups and each group will journey towards a particular direction. That's the instruction that I received from the gods."

Makuka divided the entire clan into seven groups and appointed a head. He then gave them directions. The first and second group headed up north towards the northern part of Africa, the third and fourth group journeyed through the Sinai towards the middle east, while the fifth, sixth and seventh groups went downwards towards the south east in the direction of the horn of Africa.

In another forty years, the seven groups had journeyed far and arrived in far distant lands. The first group arrived in Spain from Morocco and crossed the Atlantic to conquer the Americas. The second group journeyed upward and occupied the whole of Europe. The third ran over the Arabian Peninsula while the fourth group went into the far east, occupied the whole of India and stretched their territorial authority as far as China and Japan. The fifth group took control of the vast islands around the South China Sea. The sixth group had annexed the South Pacific islands and the seventh group took over the lands of Australia and New Zealand.

As time went by, these dark-skinned people from Africa began to experience a strange body transformation. They did not understand what was going on but realised that their offspring began to have very light skin, and curly blonde hair. The colour of their eyes also changed to green and blue. The only way that they could explain this strange phenomenon was that the curse placed upon them by their ancestors had been activated. The population grew tremendously and society expanded with people of two dominant colours. The light-skinned people saw themselves as superior to the dark-skinned because to them, they were direct descendants of the gods. This idea grew strong in their heads and soon metamorphosised into racial segregation. They ganged up and started oppressing the darker-skinned population. The abominable act of Okotoba had caught up with his descendants many centuries after he had passed. This new world grew into a racial enclave, where the colour of a man's skin was more significant than the content of his character. In those days in faraway Japan, the oppressed black population used to gather themselves together in a protest match to express their frustration to the authorities. Some of them were so creative that they spoke poetic verses in condemnation of the way they were been treated.

Human beans
Yokuatsu

You open the pot amidst flaming fire, steaming and spewing hot vapours...
Oh! My god!
Are we really not like the beans that never get cooked?
They say the goat is stubborn...
It goes back to source the very second, it's been battered and bruised...
Oh! My god!
Did you not do the same?
Are you not digging into the very hole where you've been stung?
Human beans are wise like the plant,
Though we wait for it to get cooked but it never does... So we wait...
Why wait?
Do we have that much time?
What about an alternative to war, hunger, Disease, racism, poverty, envy, covetousness, Fornication, adultery and unbelief?
Human beans...
For so many generations you have been cooked but you never get done...
How long will it take before you understand that the river gets wiser as it flows downstream...
But you, you... you... you, you, you, you...
Foolishness has become your pride
As knowledge is for the wise,
If wishes were snakes,
The ground will hitch a free ride.

Trebor continued to read the book. Every time he stopped to

do something else, he pondered over the title; *Waters of the Earth.* Whatever it denoted did not really matter at that point in time. He opened the twelfth chapter and something interesting struck him.

Meanwhile, in Africa, the imperialist culture had become strongly rooted to the ground. The entire population gradually migrated into the template proposed by the western civilisation. This was clearly demonstrated in the way they dressed, and even in the foreign language which had become the official language of communication. Religious practices had also changed. The people kind of turned their backs on their traditional way of life because it had been condemned and branded *barbaric* by the colonialists.

The political structure also passed through this fire of change. The royal institutions that the people had been used to was replaced by a western system of government where officials were either appointed by higher authorities in Europe or by local elections. The practice of democracy became the order of the day. It was strange yet worthy experiment. The people always wanted to try something new. The result was more of a curse than a blessing because the continent still remained in the dark. It was very clear that something was not adding up. A fearless African leader took this up and campaigned against it strongly. He spoke with a loud voice.

"Them all crazy is the government of the rich people, by the powerful and influential for the oppression of the poor, the less privileged and the downtrodden."

-President Sangalo Makuka.

In addition to his outspokenness, President Sangalo Makuka went a step further to express his disappointment in the entire system through a literary piece. He said…

> *Politics is like a prostitute*
> *Money dictates the style of its dance*
> *Politics' has no choice*
> *Every Tom, Dick and Harry is a partner in this game of deceitful romance*
> *Politics my ass*
> *Even politicians believe the grass is greener on the other side*
> *It's like the chameleon, changing colours to suit its appetite to hide*
> *They challenge you to walk otherwise… prove to the people how clean is your heart*
> *Will judgement day elude them?*
> *Seriously…*
> *Do you care to know why?*
> *They are the only immortal frames in the face of the earth…*
> *Chuckles, smiles, laughter, giggles…*
> *I beg, I no fit laugh*[2]

Trebor could not afford to drop the book for anything. It got more interesting and revealing as the pages flipped by.

The descendants of Makuka who were part of the lineage of Okotoba became so powerful that they succeeded in relegating their dark-skinned relatives to the background. In the modern world they controlled the territories from the east

---

[2] I've got no strength for laughter

to the west. They formed an international alliance and became a global force to reckon with. At that time, food and resources became so scarce that they needed to turn their gaze somewhere else, maybe a distant land where they could get these things in abundance and without much resistance.

They held a meeting, formed a think tank of researchers and scientists, and gave them a mandate to find a solution to the problem at hand. For several years, the group met and researched ways and means of saving a dying generation. They sent out explorers on expensive expeditions around the world. Soon, light surfaced at the end of the tunnel. Some group had spotted Africa, a virgin land with dark primitive people. The people of the new world held another important meeting where the strategies for occupation of the newly found land was perfected. A blue print on how to carry out the task was released and series of expedition were embarked upon. Both religious and political juggernauts started the race to the dark continent. All eyes were fixed on Africa; the new source of survival. This marked the beginning of the great interaction between the descendants of Okotoba, who left many centuries ago to establish distant territories and the remnants who remained in Africa. They were of the same lineage but the lighter-skinned generation who were more privileged more advanced in knowledge, did not know this or they knew but chose to ignore the reality because of their selfish intentions.

So, they descended on the motherland like a swarm of locusts. The outcome is better imagined than told in a straight narrative.

The action that followed the eagle landing on African soil was terrible, truth be told. The events that followed proved beyond all reasonable doubt that the mission of the light-skinned descendants of Okotoba was more of plundering the resources of the dark continent than helping their distant cousins to see the light. Their activities proved this fact. The action spoke louder. And their words, crafty as it seemed, were insufficient to cover their tracts. Some of their intelligent cousins saw this and spoke loudly against it. They spoke in parables and sometimes in poetic renditions. They tried so much to weaken the force that was forcing bile down their throat but were too disorganised and naïve to pull ideas potent enough to counter the rhetoric of their invading cousins. The truth about animals was that they remained animals. The only difference was that some were bigger and more powerful than the others.

Antonyms
Suck the breasts
The physician says it's healthy for you
Suck the breasts
But do not bite the nipples for your own good
Suck the breasts
Allow the cream to run down your dry throat
Suck the breasts
But never forget to stir the curves like a boat

Missionary style is an act of love
That condemns the doggy style to an act of hate
Use the scissors to cut the tape
Of virginity lost — do not ask who is to blame

Do you still want to come?
She is exhausted — tired. No extra energy to coast a home

run
No motivation for another round of fun.
The land is barren!
The trees, fruits and animals gone.
What more do you want?
Still want to go on your banging spree?
Well, there's good news for you.
There's no more virgin in the continent of the free.

The book continued to reveal things that took Trebor by surprise. He just knew that something was not adding up because what they were taught in school was very different from the things that he discovered. As he read, big questions began to ransack his already saturated brain. What did they say about the origin of man? This particular book delved a bit into the beginning. It was mind blowing. Trebor was in a hurry to read this aspect of history so that he could write another hit song. He turned another page and continued reading.

Now, this was how the beginning of the beginning began. In the beginning was nothing but the word. He it was who began everything. For Him, there was no beginning and there was never going to be an end. The light in Him shone into darkness and darkness sped away.

King I Am had set up the entire kingdom before anyone knew what he was doing. Single-handedly, he made everything before the people were awoken from their slumber. Before now, everyone existed only in his mind. By the time the veil was taken from their eyes, and they regained consciousness, they marvelled at what King I Am had done. It was wonderful, marvellous and indescribable. There was nothing that was more beautiful than his creation. The people were so contented that they just worshipped him. When all the fanfare of self-realisation had died down, King I Am allotted duties to each and everyone in the kingdom. Everyone had something to do. Some, he appointed to be cabinet ministers while others were tasked with provincial assignments. The kingdom was so large that it had no end.

Prince Lu Sotms was one of the top officials in the hierarchy of administration. He had a gigantic office in the palace. He was made the entertainment officer. By implication, his department took care of every state activity around the king. As such, he was always very close to the great King I Am. The kingdom began to flourish and grow so fast. Other smaller kingdoms were established and men of valour and integrity were appointed to oversee them. Prince Lu Sotms became swollen headed because nearly every enquiry from the people had to pass through him before they ever got to the great King. He became highly intoxicated with power and gradually began to exercise undue authority.

At this time, a new kingdom had been established and people had been sent to build a civilisation. It was far away, a place called Earthos. The people that were sent to this new world were the not-too-intelligent of the lot. They were deliberately chosen by the great king for obvious reasons. Firstly, they needed to learn how to function in this kingdom that was established on the foundation of wisdom and excellence. Secondly, mediocrity was intolerable in the enclave. So, it became very necessary to send this set of people to a place where they could evolve to the level of consciousness obtained in the great kingdom. In Earthos, they were schooled and groomed, physically and spiritually, to the level by which they could function in the great kingdom. The great kingdom only accommodated geniuses.

Prince Lu Sotms soon began to question some of the king's judgements and decisions. In no time, he subtly began to sow seeds of discord among the high-ranking officials of the central government; eventually drawing some of them to his side.

"Reason with me, Chief Thunder. How can he possess all power and authority and we're mere errand boys and servants? It's not reasonable. Absolute power corrupts"

"Very unfair," agreed chief Thunder. "Just imagine how vast this kingdom is. Will it be too much if he just allowed us to take total control of some worlds?"

"That's not my grievance, mate. I also want to be king. Seen?"

"Now, that's a tough one."

"Why? Is he not the same one that keeps stressing that nothing will be impossible to them that believe?"

The conspiracy went on unabated. Some loyal officers brought word to the king and warned him of the plans being muted by the prince. The Great King I Am said nothing. He was calm and carried on his royal duties with great confidence. The treacherous activities by Prince Lu Sotms led to a great mutiny that nearly overthrew the Great King I Am. Prince Lu Sotms mobilised his loyal lieutenants and launched an attack on the great King. It was a fierce battle. There was fire power everywhere in the kingdom. The attack was so decisive that it almost led to the end of the great dynasty of King I Am. In the end, the prince and his army of mutineers did not prevail. Although the war had devastating effects on this kingdom of light as it raged, victory finally became the portion of the Great King I Am and his loyal soldiers.

Prince Lu Sotms and all his men who were captured alive were bundled into a craft and hauled to the new kingdom, Earthos. Perhaps it was a decision aimed at giving a chance to the rebels to repent and tow the way of light. But that was never to be. As soon as he arrived with his men, things took a drastic turn for the worse. He started off his power play, in the new kingdom, manipulating the people as he wished. The reason being that he was more advanced than all of them. He became the ruler of this new kingdom by providence, and ever since, life had never been the same. He started off a campaign of hate against the great king again. The kingdom soon divided into two major peoples — those who still revered their king and those who strongly detested his ways. The followers of Prince Lu Sotms bowed to his authority and did all his biddings to the letter. The king's people were faithful even though they were persecuted and marginalised. They remained strong and bonded irrespective of the distractions. The Great King I Am kept a close eye on his subjects in Earthos and also gave a close marking on Prince Lu Sotms.

Divinity is pure,
Merciful and true
Love is gracious,
Powerful, through and through
Forgiveness is the only song in his lips
Ageless and deeper than the face of the deep

Do you look like Him?
Tell me if you dare the truth still
Throw hate and bitterness to the wind,
And let them have a bite of your fill

Blow the truth as if it were the loudest trumpet
That can never be universally silenced

At least for once, be like your papa[3]
Appear in your courts with apparels adorned with petals
Craving for righteousness
Above fake religious holiness
Making true religion live in the heart
Instead of the churchyard

All religion is one...
The bond of the father and son is strong
Love is like the morning dew
That waters the earth's food
No colours, no boundaries...
There are no versions, and no countries.

Ride not intelligence in the face of wisdom
For life is life in the sun of the kingdom

Motherland became the new heaven. Everything that the descendants of Okotoba, who had annexed the entire land needed was there. From agricultural to mineral resources. The exploitation started in earnest, from one end of the continent to the other. The seas started to boil with cargo ships that journeyed back and forth with precious and human commodities. It was the survival of the fittest. The descendants of Okotoba who had the upper hand — the western cousins —

---

[3] father

operated with impunity and plundered the continent to develop their land. Too many atrocities were committed against the indigenous people who happened to be their relatives but no authority was there to question their actions.

They established schools and churches in pursuit of an obnoxious agenda. It was more of ignorance than an act of cruelty. The result was the complete annihilation of the indigenous culture and ways of life which was replaced by the western new life. Kingdoms were destroyed and traditional institutions reduced to inconsequential. This practice of changing the people to suit their purpose continued unabated. Time went by with nothing changing. The people became confused because they saw themselves at a crossroad between their indigenous ways of life and the new ways of life imposed by their invading cousins.

Thus, the continent unwillingly hitched a ride on a pneumatic rollercoaster that had been programmed to malfunction till the end of time. It became a race against time. A time needed to inflict more damage, time to further blindfold the cash cow and on the other hand, time to pull human and natural resources together to activate the machineries of total emancipation. The descendants of Okotoba from the far north and their cousins who occupied the colonies slipped into a tug of war. It was a winner-take all kind of situation. Only time was needed to determine the direction of the pendulum.

Tick-tock is time…
Time can be likened to anything…
It has no breaks, so it cannot slow down…
It takes all forms, shapes and sizes, like a serious clown

Time is emit[4]
Time is mite
Time is meit
Time is mtei
Time is item
Time is temi
Time is tiem
Time is nothing but time.

***

Until now, no details emerged about what led Okotoba into eating the forbidden animal. The only information that shaped history was of a man who ate a forbidden animal. His action according to historical accounts brought a plague to the people and this led to a great pandemic. Another dimension of the account was that his descendants were banished from the land. The pandemic killing a lot of people to the extent that the king had to vacate his throne and went into exile. No one ever tried to shed light on Okotoba's ordeal that fateful night. He actually ate the animal against his wish all for the purpose of sustaining his civilisation. Okotoba was confronted by the spirits from beyond on that day. He ended up not hunting a game because he had to spend the entire night negotiating with the gods.

"This animal is forbidden; I cannot eat it." Okotoba continued in protest.

"We know that more than you do. You don't seem to understand what is going on here." The chief continued in

---

[4] Time spelt by inverting the letters

explanation. "Your entire civilisation will be wiped out except someone will step in to bear the burden so that the future generation can survive. You are the chosen one. You are the saviour of your generation. The gains will be far more honourable than the fangs of the pains. You will not be doing this as an act of disobedience or ignorance but an act of sacrifice… and of love."

"The consequences are enormous, my lords."

"But the gains are huge and it will run throughout all generations. Your children and your children's children will inherit the earth."

Okotoba sighed deeply and sadness descended on him like a cloak of defeat. There was no escape when the gods find you worthy. He did not need much time to think about what was been demanded of him.

"I am ready, my lords. Send me." The gods led him into the deepest part of the forest and prepared the meal for him to eat. Okotoba died as a result of the love he had for his people. There was no love that was greater than that.

***

Trebor closed the book and switched into a state of deep thought. He still had a couple of chapters to go. The good news, however, was that he had begun by now to understand the origin of his existence.

***

Nkemcho roamed the near bushes in the village hunting birds, lizards, squirrels and rabbits. Every woman and girl in the village knew him because they always came across him on every side — on bush paths, in uncompleted buildings, by the riverside, even on farmlands belonging to other people. Sometimes, he engaged them when they went to fetch water from the stream and at other times when they made their way to the farms to work or harvest their produce.

He was an easy-going lad who had no problems whatsoever. The girls loved to tease him a lot simply because of the way he reacted to them whenever their paths crossed. He possessed the technique of turning every provocation into a comic relief. Instead of getting angry at them and cursing the very day that they were born, Nkemcho would smile instead and call them his wives. He went as far as labelling the women and girls with titles such as 'wife number one, and wife number two…' and so on and so forth. This caused the girls, especially, to laugh. They giggled and enjoyed the way he played with them. Oftentimes, they stopped and stood along the road to chat with him for a long time. Sometimes, they totally forgot that they were supposed to be running errands for their respective families. Nkemcho remained the sweet boy in the girl's good books until his elder brother who lived in the city came in one day and whisked him away. He was about twelve years old when he arrived in Lagos. He continued his education in the big city and helped his brother a great deal. Every time he closed from school, he stopped by the store to conclude the day's routine by selling motor spare parts for his brother.

Ten years down the line, Nkemcho; now a mature university graduate, headed for his village for the first time in a decade. Although the excitement was unprecedented, he did not know exactly what to expect. His absence from the village for so long was due to the fact that he had lost both his parents in a communal clash between his village and another. His elder brother was so bitter and disappointed in the events that led to the killings that he decided never to return to their village. Since his elder brother was directly responsible for taking care of him, he had no choice other than to follow in his footsteps and abide by this decision.

Nkemcho descended from the motorbike that ferried him into the green landscape. It was so different from what he used to know or recollect. His mind raced back to when his mother and his uncle used to tell stories based on ancient myths. He enjoyed this period so much that his memories of these accounts remained fresh and evergreen. He particularly loved the historical account about the ancient kingdom of Owuan. The story of Okotoba filtered into his mind as he viewed the surroundings with an eye of precision. He was trying to see the exact changes that had taken place while he was away in the city.

There had been lots of development especially in the area of construction but the roads were still what they had been. They were completely deteriorated due to incessant erosion caused by unstoppable heavy rainfall. New buildings that looked very much like the ones in the big cities littered the entire landscape. Passers-by welcomed him. They knew every stranger that entered the village. They were very easy to distinguish simply by their appearance. Their clothes were always newer and better.

A curious woman approached him as he started to walk down the bush path. She walked past him and stood right in his face.

"*Nno*"[5]

"Thanks, mama."

"I'm really sorry about your mom and dad."

"That's all right, ma'am. The lord giveth and taketh. We can't question him."

"You have become a full-grown man. Your parents would have been so proud of you".

"That's life, ma". He laughed. The woman tried to refresh Nkemcho's memory of who she was by various unnecessary insinuations but Nkemcho had several feminine images in his head that he could not remember exactly who this woman was. It would have been easier to place the older woman's face if she was younger and of the same generational bubble. She walked away a bit disappointed that he could not pick her out among the many female fans that he had at the time. However, in the brief conversation, he was able to gather enough information about friends of his, both male and female, who were still in the village. This was as a result of the mention of names and compound positions of these people in question by the woman. He only needed to locate one of them and the others would naturally fall into place.

Nkemcho arrived at Ozo's compound at the east end of the village. Ozo was an old schoolmate with whom he did a lot of football-playing and game-chasing. The duo raced to Amara's house in no time. The news of his arrival was beginning to spread like wild fire. Amara was the shy one amongst the lot in those days and Ozo admired her so much. Little wonder, her house was the first point of call that he chose

---

[5] Nno - Welcome

to visit with the city boy. Amara had become very mature, beautiful and desirable.

"Ozo, where did you find this boy?"

"He found me." They laughed. Amara came closer to Nkemcho and patted him on the shoulder.

"You're now a big man and you look good — well-fed."

"And you, a big beautiful woman. I'm really glad to see you".

"Me too…"

"You used to be very shy though…"

"I'm no longer a kid."

"I see that."

They all exploded into another round of laughter.

"How long are you here for?"

"Two weeks."

"Oh, that's a lot of time to catch up."

"Definitely."

Ozo simply observed the two as they spoke. He felt a bit side-tracked and this brewed an envious sensation within him.

"I will still see you before I go back to the city."

"That will be nice."

Nkemcho and Ozo left Amara's house, stopped by a couple of houses to say hello to some people and ended up at Mama Ngozi's bar for a few drinks. Mama Ngozi's bar was the social spot where the old blended with the young. Teenagers who were in the final year of secondary education frequented the place as a sign to show that they had entered the maturity stage. It was a usually noisy place with music blasting, loud talking and drunk dancing.

The next day was market day. The village woke up much earlier in preparation for what was the biggest commercial activity of the week. Gradually, things began to fall into place as usual. Every kind of farm product; vegetables, yams, tomatoes, plantain, peppers, fruits, goats and bush meat caught by skilled hunters was on display at Ihiala market. Ozo and Nkemcho went to the market to buy some bush meat. They moved from one space into another in search of a particular game; the grasscutter. Ozo had told him that the grasscutter would be excellent to prepare pepper soup. Nkemcho received a lot of stares and sympathetic gestures from people who remembered him like it was only yesterday. This left him feeling emotional and a bit sad but it was quite understandable because being sympathetic formed a great part of the people's way of life. The bargain was quick and straight to the point. Nkemcho reached for his wallet at the same time that Ozo bent over to pick up the grasscutter. A gentle touch at his back made him jump around. He thought it was a pick-pocket. That smile on her face was all he needed.

"Amara. So, it's you?"

"Yes…"

"I thought it was some thief."

"Thief in this village? No way. You're safe"

"Amara you're in the market again today." Ozo cut in.

"I don't miss it. It is either I'm here to sell or to buy." Nkemcho zeroed into Amara's stunning frame. He liked everything he saw.

"Amara. We're doing grasscutter pepper soup tonight. You're invited." The smile on his face was enough to make it an irresistible offer.

"Oh, that's a nice one. It would be interesting to taste the men's cuisine."

"We're better cooks, you know."

"Your opinion."

"It's a statement of fact."

"We'll see." She smiled. "Take care guys and see you in the evening."

Ozo led the way as they squeezed through a wall of people. Amara disappeared in the crowd. Nkemcho and Ozo soon moved away from the noise and crowd and through a lonely bush path, they vanished into the shrubs.

The smell of delicious pepper soup enveloped Ozo's back house apartment. The aroma of the scent leaf was quite strong. A cloud of smoke gushed out of the fire he had made with dry wood pieces that his mother had fetched from the farm earlier in the morning. Ozo sat on a small stool near the fireplace and stirred the content in the blackened pot. Then he raised his head and looked at Nkemcho.

"You shouldn't have invited that girl."

"Why?"

"She will not come."

"Why won't she come?"

"Her parents will never allow her to walk at nights. I invited her so many times for a walk but she never made it. Every time I see her the next day, her parents were always to blame because they just won't allow her."

"It's all right. Whether she comes or not, it won't stop us from demolishing this pot of pepper soup tonight." The laughter was short-lived.

Ozo's mother appeared from the corner of the house to see what the boys were up to. The smile on her face was that of joy. She enjoyed every process of growth that her son had to pass through. Now, he looked strong and agile. Ozo used to be a very sickly child. It was claimed that his grandfather who was a Sickler re-incarnated in him. The man used to be a very sick man during his lifetime. The people believed so much in people dying and coming back to live again. The belief was so sacred that whenever someone died, a mark was grafted in a particular part of the individuals' body as a proof to authenticate their claim. As the practice was, newly born babies were quickly scrutinised to ascertain which dead family member had come back to life.

Ozo's mother teased the boys about their cooking. She reminded them that it was a woman's responsibility to cook.

"I know what that means." Ozo shot at her mother. "Don't worry, we will get married when the time is right."

"By the special grace of God." She prayed. It was every mother's desire to see their children get married and start up a family. Ozo's mother was one of the many women who believed that responsibility in a man only began after he had found a wife. "Don't forget to send my portion of the pepper soup."

"That's okay, Mama," they almost replied at the same time.

Then she made her way out.

Her exit coincided with the appearance of a familiar figure from the distance. Ozo followed Nkemcho's gaze until it landed on the queen. She was so smooth, clean and beautiful. Nkemcho simply smiled. The arrival of Amara changed the atmosphere. It was of excitement and jealousy. Nkemcho was happy to see that she honoured the invitation while Ozo thought that Amara was unfair to him. It was clear that she preferred the guy from the city to the village boy. Nkemcho quickly turned to Ozo.

"I thought you said that she will not come." Ozo's

response was a deep sigh.

Amara walked majestically towards the boys whose eyes were now busy dissecting her anatomy in very lustful ways.

"Hi guys," she smiled as she approached the boys. Ozo's jaws dropped. He had not seen a girl so beautiful since he arrived. Nkemcho took a step forward and stretched forth his hands.

"You look stunning."

"Thank you." She cast a careless glance at Ozo and returned her focus on Nkemcho. "Hope you guys are doing good?"

"Yes, we are. Thank you."

Ozo raised his head from the fire spot and gave a quick sign to Nkemcho. He grabbed the meaning at once. He turned to Amara and signalled to her.

"Come inside, beautiful."

Ozo's room was a large one. A small sized mattress on the floor, a reading table on the side near the window and a wardrobe made of soft tarpaulin. The blue colour of the wardrobe was a brilliant one. It was the first thing that hit the eyes of anyone who entered the room. Amara noticed the shine almost immediately. The room smelled of mud and white clay. These two locally sourced products were very important materials that were used to polish the rooms and keep bad odours away. The transistor radio on the table was very old. The silver antenna was broken and Ozo had to improvise a method of keeping it in contact with the other half. The fluctuation of the soundwave that emanated from the speaker was largely due to the broken antenna. As a result of this, the sound from the radio did more harm than good to the ears. Amara sat on the mattress with both legs positioned sideways the left resting on the right. The multi-coloured dress that she wore was very short. Girls were taught how to sit properly to avoid the exposure of their private areas. It was so natural for the man's eyes to pan into an open leg of any woman. The dignity and pride of womanhood in those days was hidden between their legs. Amara scanned the entire room once more and finally fixed her gaze on the radio. Nkemcho focussed on her all the time while Ozo boiled with jealousy but he did not show it.

"Enjoy your soup," said Ozo pushing the bowl in front of the girl.

"Thank you very much."

Nkemcho stared at Amara and smiled.

"Nkemcho, eat your meal. You just keep staring at the girl. You want her to be shy?"

"Far from it, Ozo. I'm just admiring her."

"It's enough. Let's enjoy our pepper soup."

Amara observed the boys as the argued and smiled. The spoon in her hands trembled slightly. Gradually, she lowered the spoon into the bowl and lifted a scoop. Then she sipped slowly to avoid getting her lips burnt. She dipped the spoon again into the bowl and brought out a large chunk of meat. Then she began to chew the meat. The steam from the blue plastic bowl created a circling effect in the room. Nkemcho was sitting on the reading chair while Ozo sat on bare floor. Streams of sweat ran down their foreheads as they ate. Nkemcho's nose dripped as a result of the spices in the pepper soup. He was not a fan of hot peppers. For about five minutes, no one made a sound. Finally, the long silence was broken by no other than their female guest.

"This is really good." Amara did enjoy every bit of the

eating experience. "Who made this?"

"Me of course. Who else? You don't expect this novice from the city to know anything about pepper soup cooking. He's been away from this village, it's now over ten years." They laughed.

"It tastes really delicious."

"Thank you, Amara. I accept the compliment." The trio discussed through and after the dinner time, deliberating mainly on education and family. Nkemcho was the lucky one because he was out of university and was already gainfully employed. Amara and Ozo were still not sure about furthering their educational ambition due to financial difficulties.

Later that evening, Nkemcho walked Amara back to her house. They continued to talk about school and future plans. Amara wanted to go to the university but her parents could not afford the tuition.

"You're lucky."

"Yea. My brother really tried for me. He saw me through the university without sweat. I am forever grateful to him."

"He's a good man."

There ensued a brief silence.

"I feel for you, though," he came back alive.

"Such is life. But we will survive. They're asking me to get married."

"Hmmm... that's not a bad idea."

"Are you serious?"

"No. I was only joking." Then he took her hand and smiled down at her. He was much taller than her. "Seriously, I think the marriage thing could be a much more practical way out."

"You can't be serious, Nkem."

"Yet, I am. What if I make you an offer?"

Amara burst into laughter. It was not clear what was really funny. Then she looked up at Nkemcho smiling like a child in front of a chocolate rack.

"What's the offer?" Nkemcho took her by the hand and they started to walk again. Then he dropped the bomb. It came like a two hundred kilo punch. She was not expecting it.

"Marry me and I will send you to the university."

"You're joking." Amara snapped.

"I'm serious. I just got a job in the city. I'm here because I need a wife. I have loved you Amara for always."

"My God!"

"Seriously. I was too young to understand that what I felt for you was indeed real love."

"This is a big shock to me. But it's very touching."

"I know."

"Hmm... I will still have to talk to my parents, anyways."

"That's okay. They will be excited I believe."

"Are you pulling my legs or what?"

"Not at this moment. You will make them happy if you fulfil their dreams."

"Yeah. But it's not just about getting married, you know."

"How do you mean?"

"It will now be more about the person."

"I see. But does that depend on them? Are you not the one to make the decision about the person?"

"Yes and no. Yes, because if I like the guy, I will gladly accept. And no because if my parents don't want him, that will create a lot of tension in the family. See where I'm coming from?"

"Yea, yea... Anyways, I'm still around. Take your time

and reflect on our chat tonight. Then let me know what you think."

She smiled and looked at him. There was an unmistakable affection written all over her beautiful face.

"I will. Goodnight and see you tomorrow."

"Sweet dreams, my dear." She left him rooted to the spot. Amara turned around to leave but Nkemcho pulled her back and hugged her. He watched the beautiful Amara disappear into the distance. As he turned around to go, he bumped into Ozo. He had been trailing their movement since they left the house.

"You didn't discuss this plan with me." His face was coloured with bitterness.

"Come, my friend. You need to stop eavesdropping."

"You are trespassing on another man's territory."

"Another man's territory? And who's this other man?"

"Nkemcho. I was there before you came in. I have indicated my interest in this girl and we've been on for the past three years now. You think you can just come and take her away from me?"

"I don't get you, Ozo. The girl is not saying anything about you and her having a relationship."

"That doesn't matter. Just stay away from her."

"Really?"

"Yes!"

"Okay. Let's go."

They walked home together without saying a single word to each other. Nkemcho felt very uneasy due to the development. He began to think of what to do. He thought first of leaving Ozo's house to another location. But it was about too late to initiate the move because he had to make an alternative arrangement. However, he decided to pass the night in Ozo's house. The rivalry created a negative aura around them and Nkemcho felt this was dangerous. He tried to ease the tension in order to perfect his plan by having a quick chat with his friend.

"Ozo, let's talk man to man. Honestly, I never knew that two of you are having an affair. But it's all right now that you have told me. I'm sorry if I hurt you."

"That's fine."

"Thanks', my brother. It's not healthy for us to be having this misunderstanding over a girl."

"I know. I'm sorry too."

Ozo felt better as it seemed his friend had accepted defeat. They slept that night in peace. The next morning, Nkemcho left Ozo's house. He ended up in his cousin's place that was very far from the village. Although, he found it a bit worrisome, he had no choice. It was uncomfortable because he had to travel a long distance every time, he needed to see Amara.

It had been over one week since Nkemcho left Ozo's place. He continued to visit Amara on a daily basis. One day, Nkemcho was coming from the girl's house when Ozo intercepted him.

"You're a devil. So, you think that I don't know that you've been visiting my girl on a daily basis?"

"Ozo, I don't understand what your problem is. The girl said she's not having an affair with you."

"That's a lie, you betrayer. What do you expect her to tell you? Must she drum the truth into your ears before you know? Don't you have eyes?"

"Okay, I need to get over with this once and for all. Let's

go her house right now and clear the air."

"Let's go. You think I'm afraid to go there?" The sudden arrival of Amara at the scene of the argument aggravated the already heated atmosphere.

"What's going on here?"

"Please ask him," said Nkemcho with a wave of the hand.

"Ozo."

"Amara, I've been keeping quiet since all these days. What do you think you're doing with Nkemcho?"

"And what type of question is that? I don't understand."

Nkemcho quickly stepped into the picture.

"Listen. Ozo has been accusing me of snatching you from him. He said you guys are dating. I told you this the other day but you denied it."

"I told you the truth. We're not dating. We're just friends."

Nkemcho turned to Ozo. His eyes were wide open.

"See… She said there's nothing like you and him dating. Is that clear now?"

"Amara, is this the way you want to treat me? Just because of this city boy you forgot everything that we shared?"

"Please, Ozo. You have to stop this. I never had an affair with you and you know it."

"Peter denied Jesus. So, I'm not surprised. But you will pay for this big betrayal." He hurried away and left the new lovers on the spot, staring at each other.

"I don't get this, Amara. Please, tell me the truth."

"I am telling you the truth. I have never dated Ozo and I will never do. Believe me."

"If you say so."

"He's jealous of the fact that I'm inclined towards you. It's true he's been making passes at me for years but I don't want to be with him. It's you I need."

Nkemcho pulled Amara to his chest and hugged her passionately.

"Thank you, darling."

"Why? There's nothing to thank me for. We're both in this together."

"True."

Amara smiled. It was a triumphant one.

"Let me accompany you." They started walking towards the market square where Nkemcho was billed to hire a bike.

"Could you believe it was your argument that brought me out. Your voices were so loud and I could hear my name being mentioned."

"Really?"

"Yeah."

Nkemcho shook his head disappointedly, threw his hand round her neck and slowly dragged her along the way.

Amara and Nkemcho's relationship which started dramatically led them into part of a marital journey. Everything happened so fast. The marriage between the young couple took place just a few months later. The entire village experienced a festival-like ceremony on their wedding day. Every one, except Ozo, stood behind their back and supported them in every way that they could. It was a show of true love and solidarity. The couple was so happy that they found each other. To them, marriage was not only beautiful, it was the most perfect thing under the sun. They spent a couple of days in the village after the ceremony to relax and appreciate the love that the people showed to them. Afterwards, they left for the city where Nkemcho worked in an oil servicing company as a system engineer.

Amara got into the university as promised by her husband. He bought her a small car for commuting because she had to attend lectures from home. She juggled her responsibility as a wife and also as student quite well. The house was peaceful and the couple danced in the euphoria of true happiness. This was a union made in heaven.

Amara was an academic. She loved to study a lot. Her course mates called her 'Madam Professor'. She was one of the brightest students in the mass communication class. As a leader, she formed study groups that helped the entire class in their academic pursuit. She was brains and beauty put together.

Amara did not get pregnant and this became a big worry for her husband. They tried everything that money could afford but it did not happen. Amara became depressed. The happiness that she had found in getting married to the man of her dreams began to turn sour. It was her third year in university. This development brought a lot of distraction that largely contributed to the drastic drop in her grades. She often sat alone under a mango tree behind the faculty building lost in thought. Someone in her class had noticed this behaviour and wanted to know what this was all about.

"Madam, you've been here for a long time now. Is anything the matter?" Romeo was Amara's course mate. They were friends and sometimes studied together in the library.

"I'm okay, Romeo."

"You don't look it. Is there anything that I can do?"

"No. Thanks. It's very kind of you. I should be leaving now."

"Are you sure you're ready to go now?"

"I can give you a ride if that's why you're asking." She smiled.

"Let me quickly get my folder from the class then."

Romeo ran off. Amara stared in the direction that he went but she was actually not looking at him. She was physically in the place but she was lost in space. Her thought lacked adequate light capable of illuminating the world around her.

Nkemcho arrived home from work to discover that Amara was not back from school. It was very unusual. He sluggishly went to the kitchen to get a cold drink. The television came on as he sank into the brown leather sofa. He had switched it on as soon as he came into the house. He loosened his tie and fixed his gaze at a breaking news from CNN.

Traffic was quite heavy. It took Amara a longer time to get to the bus stop where Romeo could get another vehicle home. She pulled over after waiting a couple of seconds for a commercial vehicle to depart.

"I suggest you take things easy, madam."

"I will. It's just that I've got lots of things in my head lately. I will get over them soon. Thanks."

"I'm always available to help, madam. Thanks for the ride."

"Don't mention it. See you tomorrow." He shut the door gently and Amara sped off into the double carriageway.

Amara opened the door to find her husband had dozed off over the news channel. She observed him carefully and then advanced with the intention of waking him up. But before she could touch him, he opened his eyes.

"Oh dear. I thought you were sleeping."

"Where are you coming from?"

"School of course."

"What time is it?"

"I'm sorry, I'm late. The traffic was hectic."

"The traffic will always take the blame I know."

"Yes. I'm sorry. I will quickly fix us something for dinner."

"I'm not hungry."

"Have you eaten something?"

"I'm not hungry, madam." His voice was loud and very cold. Then he stood up and walked into the bedroom. Amara remained in the same spot for a minute before making her way to the room where he had entered. She found Nkemcho lying on the bed with his legs on the floor. She knew something was not adding up. She moved over to him slowly and sat at the edge of the bed.

"Honey, what's the matter? You're not looking good tonight."

"You are my problem, Amara. It's almost four years in this marriage and no child. You think that I'm happy about it?"

"I'm not happy either but it's not my fault. I am not God."

"Oh, it's my fault…"

"I didn't say that."

"Just leave me alone."

"Honey…"

"Please…"

"Okay, okay, okay… I'm in the kitchen if you need me." Amara walked back into the living room and sat down dejectedly. The clock ticked on and time was waiting for no one. The situation had created an atmosphere of bitterness around the couple. The sweet love she thought was hers had finally gone sour.

The next day after late morning lectures, Romeo found Amara sitting on a bench in the same spot as the previous day. She was in total isolation from the campus hustle and bustle.

For her, the mango tree provided a perfect shelter from the sporadic attack of life's hailstones. She kept having this deep feeling that everything was going to be okay, yet she was so uneasy. Romeo advanced quickly to the spot and sat beside her. He leaned forward to look at her face. It was then he discovered streams of tears rolling down her cheeks.

"You're here again, madam."

"Yea…"

"Are you okay?"

"I think I am."

"No, you're not."

"I'll be fine, Romeo."

Romeo sat close to her for a couple of minutes without saying a word. Amara simply kept her head straight and stared into empty space.

"Come with me."

"Why?"

"Just come. You need to be out of here for a while. Where's your car key?"

All Amara could do was to look at the man beside her taking charge of affairs. She felt like a dumb person being led by the nose. Romeo pulled her up gently and led her to where her car was parked about seventy metres away. He helped her to sit in the passengers' side and shut the door carefully. Romeo went over to the other side and sat in the driver's seat. Then he made a move to start the engine.

"You're not insured to drive my car, Romeo."

"Don't worry about that."

Romeo started the car and drove out of the university campus to an unknown destination. It was a quiet restaurant on the outskirts of town. It appeared very posh by its structure, lavish furnishings and decoration, and also by the calibre of cars that were parked within the premises.

"Where are we?"

"This place is called *D Yummiz*. They serve the best African dishes in the entire locality. Listen… I didn't like the way you were looking a while back. I thought you needed a change of scene so I decided we could have a good lunch together."

"Very kind of you, Romeo?"

"It's all right."

"Tell me, was it very obvious that something was wrong with me?"

"I noticed. But I don't know about other people."

"I really appreciate it. Thank you so much."

"Don't mention it. Come, let's go and eat good native food."

Romeo and Amara had a delicious lunch and retired to the side garden to cool off. There were a couple of round tables in the area. Some had two chairs and others four. Romeo and Amara settled at the table with two chairs and glanced at the plastic menu in front of them.

"What are you drinking?"

"Wine, maybe… red."

"Any small chops to go with it?"

"No, thanks. I'm full to the brim."

"Okay then. I will be right back." Romeo left and Amara cocooned herself in her thoughts once more. A wholesome five minutes ticked by. She did not notice Romeo's presence until he placed the two glasses filled with red wine on the table.

"Thanks."

"It's my pleasure."

Amara rushed down the content in the glass to Romeo's amazement.

"You like it."

"Yeah. It's a smooth red. I love them like that. I think a second glass will just be perfect." She winked at Romeo.

"Don't forget you will be driving home alone."

"I know. But prepare to drive me home if I'm not able to."

They laughed. Romeo felt a great satisfaction from the fact that she was loosening up.

"Hmm... Your wish, madam." Romeo ran off again to get Amara a second glass of wine. He came back much earlier this time. They sipped from the glasses in front of them and talked mainly of school. Amara felt relieved from the burden she had been carrying for some time now.

"I'm already running late, Romeo. I need to get home before my husband arrives."

They left the garden lounge and headed to where the car was parked. Romeo drove Amara home that evening. This became a regular practice as both of them hung out quite often. Amara had found solace in excessive wine drinking in the company of a younger male friend. One evening, her husband saw Romeo getting out of the car and Amara taking the driver's seat a few metres from the house. He was so furious but he managed to keep a calm face.

"I reckon you now have a driver?"

"No. Why?"

"I thought I saw a man getting out of the driver's seat in your car?"

"Yea. He's my course mate. I was a bit tipsy after drinking some red wine in school. I didn't want to risk it."

"OK. I thought you would have been thinking of how to

get me a child instead of turning yourself into an overnight alcoholic."

"Honey…"

"Stop! Don't patronize me."

"Babe, the doctor said there's nothing wrong with me…"

"What are you insinuating?"

"… Nothing!"

That night was the most horrible night she ever had since they got married. They quarrelled till the early hours of the next day.

The next morning, she drove to school in tears. On her way, she called Romeo to find out if he was in school already. The phone was engaged so she continued to try until the line went through.

"Where are you? I've been trying to call since… Are you in school, already."

"No, I'm still home."

"Okay, I'll come pick you up."

Amara drove another thirty-five minutes to Romeo's house very close to the same restaurant where they had gone to eat on the day that she was down. They normally went there to chill. She met Romeo at the gate waiting to let her into the block of flats. There was a long gate that opened inwards to the compound. He signalled to her to drive in and park near a huge water tank. Then he walked quickly to the car, opened the door for her to get out, and then ushered her through a door that led to the staircase.

His room was lavishly furnished far above the level of a university student. He had everything in the right place; nice leather furniture, modern electronic gadgets and beautiful decorative ornaments. The guy had good taste for aesthetics.

Amara felt very comfortable in this one room self-contained apartment. Romeo disappeared into the room and left her to savour the beauty of his abode. By the time he came back in, Amara was standing near the bookshelf staring at an old photo frame that was sitting on the top left corner of the shelf. Romeo slipped behind her to see what she was engrossed in.

"Oh... That's me and my family."

"Hmm... It's a very nice souvenir."

"Thanks... By the way what do I offer you, madam?"

"Stop, Romeo. Don't call me madam."

Amara brushed past him and collapsed on the sofa. Romeo followed and sat in a single chair on the side near the entrance door.

"But why?"

"It makes me feel old."

He laughed.

"Aren't you old?"

"Am I?"

"No, you're not... Just teasing. Let me get you the usual."

Another hour had passed. Amara was very relaxed. They drank red wine and ate peanuts. The reality show program on television had held Amara captive. She enjoyed watching TV especially programs that had love related themes. The love scenes in the program that she was watching were so erotic that she got totally carried away. She did not realize how fast the time was rolling by. It did not really matter as her body language did not show of one who was in a hurry to go anywhere. Romeo maintained his position, his eyes on the four-sided box. He sipped from his cup more often than the woman and secretly spied on her.

"Can I use the rest room, please?"

"Oh, yes. I'll show you." Romeo quickly jumped to his feet. Amara stood up and followed behind him and they walked through the link door leading to his room. As he approached the door leading to the rest room, he stopped and turned to her.

"This way... ."

It happened so fast. Amara grabbed Romeo's shirt, pulled him to the spot where she stood and planted a kiss on his lips. Romeo was shocked. They stared into each other's eyes for a few seconds and then started to kiss. It lasted a couple of minutes. Then Romeo broke away, guilt written all over his face.

"I'm sorry, madam." He looked away and she smiled. It was clear that she was a bit tipsy.

Amara stood motionless, her focus still on Romeo, lusting over his masculine frame. Then he turned his head away. It was the moment of decision. By the time his focus returned, his eyes landed on her cleavage. His eyes were steadily concentrated on her partly exposed breasts.

"I'm sorry. I shouldn't have done this. It's my fault." Then she turned away and stepped into the rest room. Romeo could not think straight. He just stood at the door of the toilet and waited. She emerged from the toilet after a couple of minutes and met Romeo waiting at the door. She smiled and confronted him.

"What are you doing here?"

"Waiting for you of course."

"You're not serious. What for?" said Amara as she adjusted her shirt button. Then she tried to squeeze herself past his broad frame. Romeo grabbed her and pulled her in.

"Oh, my God," she breathed under his nose. Their lips

touched and he began to kiss her deeply. He kissed her so hard that she started to moan. Then, he broke off.

"You want it, don't you? That's what you've always wanted, right."

"Yes, Romeo. Take me. Give me all you've got"

They got locked again in a long kiss that ended in an explosive love-making session.

Amara and Romeo started to skip classes. The need to satisfy their appetite for passionate love-making took centre stage. This development catapulted the lovers in a spiral that blossomed into a full-fledged love affair. The crack in Amara's marriage widened and deteriorated by the day. The couple existed as one in the same space but they were far from each other as far as the marital obligations that they both agreed to adhere to were concerned. Their love life was seriously affected by this situation. They hardly made love like before. When they did, it was not magical. Most times, Amara had to force her way through to her husband. This anomaly continued for several weeks until the day that she announced to Nkemcho that she was pregnant. It came as a great relief. Joy and peace gradually returned to the house. The tension in the marriage died down very quickly. Apologies started to fly from left, right and centre.

"My darling, I'm so sorry. I was so frustrated." Nkemcho apologised.

"It's all right, honey. I forgive you. Forgive me too."

"I can't believe this. We're going to have a baby?" The excitement in his eyes brewed sparkles of light.

"God is good. He's ever faithful."

"Honestly…"

Nkemcho made an immediate arrangement for an interior

designer to visit the house. The preparation for the arrival of the baby was in top gear. The third bedroom in the house was automatically transformed into a lavishly furnished kiddie's bedroom. He pampered Amara to a fault and regretted all the ill-treatment he meted out to her when the going was tough and rough. Life returned to normal, the exact way that it began. Amara took off time from school to avoid any sort of complication. She gave Romeo a considerable distance as she did not want to complicate matters any longer. They kept talking on the phone but hardly hooked up like before. Everything went on smoothly until she was due.

The private clinic where Nkemcho and his wife received medical attention was a first-class facility. His employers took care of their medical bills. They had three medical facilities like that in the city where their staff were adequately taken care of whenever they fell ill. Nkemcho checked his wife into the maternity ward and hurried home to get some materials that he had forgotten to carry along. They had rushed to the clinic as a matter of urgency when the labour pains increased early that morning. It did not take long to pack the remainder of the baby's stuff into a bag. He dashed out of the house and drove off at high speed. Nkemcho tried to manoeuvre his Mercedes Benz car through the hectic traffic. It was the usual bumper to bumper style of congestion. Unfortunately for him, there were no side roads where he could have taken some short cuts. The frustration grew as time slipped. He needed to get back to the hospital as fast as he could. He just wanted to be by his wife when the baby was delivered. He found this necessary because his wife was very fragile. His presence in that place would make a big difference. The radio played a smooth jam. That helped in calming his nerves but his heart was pounding strongly. It took thrice the amount of time that it would have taken for him to get back to the hospital. On arrival, he parked his car in the first available space which was meant for disabled drivers. On getting to the reception, he went in the direction of the staircase. He could not wait for the lift to take him to the second floor where his wife was kept. Nkemcho raced up the stairs avoiding mostly people who were descending from the top floors. His hands trembled as he pulled the door knob after a voice had asked him to come in. He opened the door and saw his wife clutching a newly born baby on her chest. A voice greeted him from a far corner. It was a nurse in light blue uniform.

"Congratulations, sir. It's a baby boy."

"Thank God... And thank you too."

He went to the side of the bed and planted a kiss on Amara's lips.

"You took so long," she said.

"I'm sorry. It was the traffic."

"Traffic always takes the blame."

They laugh.

"I love you, baby. You are brave."

"Hmm... Thank you."

"How's the baby doing?"

He turned around the other way to catch a glimpse of the baby's face.

"He's doing great."

"I don't really know how to carry a newly born baby. I always feel I'm going to let them fall."

"I understand. You have a lot of time. Babies grow very fast."

Another nursing sister brought in a file that he handed

over to Nkemcho to sign. He spent about an hour with his wife and child before heading to the office. In the evening, he was back at the hospital. An hour later, his wife was discharged and he drove them home a happy man.

Amara had three kids in all; two boys and a girl. The family situation was enviable. Everyone was happy and the kids were doing very well. Nkemcho had initiated a relocation project which was successful. The entire family was to move to the United States of America. As one of the procedures, the DNA of the kids were needed to further process the application. On this day, he went to get the results.

Amara was home with the children after they came back from school. She was busy trying to settle them down when her phone began to ring. She hurriedly dropped the kiddies school bags in her hand and raced back to the living room where her handbag was lying carelessly on the sofa.

"Hi."

The voice on the other end was masculine. It was indeed Romeo.

"I've called so many times. You didn't pick up."

"Yes, I know. I've been busy with the kids... listen, I will call you back as soon as I'm free." She hung up. As she made her way to the stairs, her phone rang again. She just looked at it and moved on.

Nkemcho stared unbelievably at the man in front of him.

"This cannot be possible."

"But that's it, sir. Our results are mostly accurate."

Nkemcho sighed and sank into a chair nearby. Then he reached for his phone again and dialled a number. The person on the other end did not pick the phone. He managed to stand up and slowly, he made his way to the car and drove off.

Amara settled the kids at the dining table with their lunch and came back to the living room. She picked up her phone and checked the missed calls. Her husband had been trying to reach her. She dialled her husband's number and waited for him to pick up. The phone rang several times and stopped. She picked up the remote control and turned on the television.

Nkemcho arrived home after a forty minutes' drive. He dragged his feet until he got into the house. The kids had all retired to their rooms. Amara walked to him to welcome him with the customary kiss but he just brushed her aside and went into the room. She followed him because she knew something was wrong.

"Darling, what is it again?"

Nkemcho stared at her in silence. Amara was confused. She did not know what to do. Then she advanced towards him and sat on the bed. Her heart began to beat uncontrollably. She was not in any way ready to go down that lane the second time. Then her eyes caught the brown envelope on the bed. She looked at it and remembered where her husband had gone to. It almost gave her a heart attack. She looked up and managed to stare at her husband in the face.

"Amara... why? Why?"

"My husband..."

"No..."

"I don't..."

"Who's the father to those kids you call mine?"

Then it dawned on her that it was about the DNA result. Then she opened the envelope. Her hands trembled.

"My God!"

"Your God, what? So, you've been cheating on me, Amara?"

"It's not what you think…"

"Then what is it? The three kids are not mine!"

"There must… there must be… some mistake…"

"Shut the fuck up, woman. In this age of advanced tech?"

"Take it easy, Nkem."

"I demand to know… who is the father of those kids?"

Amara stammered. The words refused to come.

So, things fell apart. None of the children belonged to Nkemcho. He was devastated. He did not know whether to live or to die. Everything about life, love and happiness got blown into the air like a nuclear bomb. Nkemcho cried till the tears ran dry. Amara moved out of the house immediately, and took the kids along. Love that was so sweet had suddenly turned not only sour but poisonous. Nkemcho soliloquised randomly to ease his confused mind. The words were heavy…

Let me love you today.
And if tomorrow ever come, spit in its face
Hold on to me, never let me go
Burn me up in your warm embrace.

Fantastic words only will I speak
As truth is nowhere to be found
You were not the angel I thought,
The delight that I always wanted to have around

Then, loving you was till the end of time
And I said till death do us part
Your happiness remained my obligation
Now see who laughs last

Between two of us, who is the devil?
A stranger crawled into my house
I cannot sleep with two eyes closed
Love has turned into a vicious count

How I do not believe in love but I believe in God
We do not come in two but in one
That's why fantastic words don't stand
The honourable test of time.

Nkemcho went through a long process of healing. He quit his job in the oil servicing company. The shame was too much to manage. Later that year, he joined the leading political party in the country. He needed to do something very different that would help in erasing the bad memories of the past. His ambition was to contest for a seat in the federal house of representatives. About his estranged wife, he heard nothing and that was good for him. He accepted to be the secretary of the youth wing, a position that was loaded with enormous responsibilities. He was in charge of mobilisation of the youth at grassroots level at all times, especially during political activities. He also took to reading books especially historical accounts of great politicians. Nkemcho was reading a book about an African leader who gave his life for the wellbeing of his people. This story fascinated him so much because he discovered another way of expressing love. For him, to give love to the society was much more profitable and fulfilling than giving to one person. It was a weird belief but he felt very comfortable with it, looking back to what happened between him and his estranged wife.

The life of Zan Gusto as recorded in the book became a

source of inspiration to him. The book was always in his hands. He read it any time he was free. It was Monday evening after a series of caucus meetings with officials of the party at the local government level. He settled down in his bed after a light dinner of Italian-style salad on seabass grilled fish. Then he picked up the book again and began to read.

The land was massive. It covered from the east coast of the Indian ocean to the west coast of the Atlantic, spreading across an entire continent. To the north lived the wandering Tulani of north African descent, and the south was bothered by the unconquerable Zuluani. In all, Motema remained a stable country. President Zan Gusto, was the great grandson of President Zango Makuka. As a young dynamic military officer, he overthrew the government of John Rumala, whom they claimed was an ally of the imperialist western invaders from Europe. Zan Gusto was a complete nationalist who cared only about the welfare of his people and the importance of peaceful co-existence with others.

For six and a half years, he had single-handedly transformed the fortunes of his country, and turned it into a self-reliant and self-sufficient nation. Every sector of the economy functioned at least to an agreeable level. The extent of developmental success was breath-taking. There was abundant food in the land and the people were happy with their lives because the unemployment rate was less than three percent. They loved President Zan Gusto simply because he was a selfless and detribalised leader. He initiated an economic recovery policy that put the country on the path to greatness. He built an extensive housing project, for instance, that took care of every citizen. Essential food items were distributed to the entire population during every festivity. He made sure that every graduate from the university had a steady job as soon as they left school. The country was adorned with good roads, great infrastructure like standard hospitals, educational institutions of international repute and social welfare that competed with its counterparts in the west. Every married couple was given a grant of fifty thousand dollars to start up their lives and children under the age of eighteen were entitled to child benefit. The resources of the country which came mainly from crude oil, diamonds and gold amongst other hard minerals was distributed evenly to cater for all its citizens and their needs. The country was booming with growth to the envy of all and sundry.

The neighbouring nations within the enclave began a race of time. Every leader wanted to be like Zan Gusto. His achievements became a standard for all the leaders within and outside the continent. He was so charismatic and he spoke with great passion. His dream was to bring together all mankind under one umbrella; because according to him, humanity could only thrive under the same goals and ideologies.

On the other side of the world, Zan Gusto was a bad leader who did not allow his people the freedom to have a say in the issues of governance. Thus, they began to spread a propaganda of hate and discredited his government. Spies were sent to the country to monitor everything he was up to and to sow seeds of discord amongst the people. He did intercept a number of them but they kept on trooping in. Zan Gusto held his ground and matched his detractors, word for word, foot by foot. The powers from the west did not like this audacious character in Zan Gusto and they were in a hurry to get rid of him. All efforts to get him out of power failed. Something drastic and decisive had to be done. He seemed to be standing in the way of a global authority and this they did not appreciate.

A secret meeting was held to discuss Zan Gusto's policies and how they were detrimental to the development and growth of the global powers who controlled the political and economic landscape of the planet. It was a crucial one and an agreement was to be reached on how to take care of the situation.

"President Zan Gusto is confronting the authority of the Super 8 by not following laid down guidelines and procedures on good governance. We have given him more than enough time to adjust but he had remained adamant. It is time to sort him out once and for all." The leader of the world powers concluded. The idea was that he had to be shown the way out of power.

"We've tried every possible option and they didn't seem to work. I don't see what else we can do than to watch out for some kind of opportunity to achieve this objective." The leader of the free nation added.

"I spoke extensively to one of our top scientists and great thinker. He seemed to have an idea on what we can do to take care of this situation. Delay is dangerous. Every material needed for new technological development and production is sourced from this country. If we do not take absolute control of events and happenings there, it may stall our growth and our tight grip on global authority and economy."

"Exactly what idea did you discuss with him?" Mr Li Marcos was from an island nation in south east Asia.

"It's a two-point strategy. One is a laboratory sting to cause an epidemic scare, and two the introduction of a strong opposition in the midst of the chaos."

"And if that doesn't work?"

"Then we will be forced to invent some cogent reason to attack the country and help a willing military officer take advantage of the situation. It has to be someone we trust who will always do our bidding."

"This is evil." Mr Mpenzi was the only African leader in the Super 8.

"There's nothing like evil, your excellency. Evil does not exist. Only good. Everything we're doing here is for the good of humanity."

"I don't understand why you would want to replace a leader who's doing great stuff for his people," argued President Mpenzi.

"It is about our survival. Don't take it personally. If the lion plays good boy with the antelope, his reward will be death by starvation. It's a choice that we must make."

"But can't we all evolve together with each entity given the opportunity and support to advance at their own pace?"

"That will be to our disadvantage. If they become too conscious of what they have and manage to gain control of it all, and then know how to use them, we will be in serious trouble. In fact, if it were morally possible, eliminating the entire race and running over their land would have been the best option."

"Really?"

"Yes. Really."

"Do you realise that I'm an African?"

"I know that. We are looking at a bigger picture here. Your being African has got nothing to do with it."

The heat of blackmail, physical and psychological aggression began to mount on Zan Gusto from the Super 8 and their collaborators. The country soon began to witness unimaginable sanctions and sabotage from both within and outside the country. The intensity of this plot to oust the president gradually began to weaken his grip on power as some of his trusted friends began to openly criticize his policies. The heat of betrayal gradually closed in on him. A number of occasions, he would retire to the penthouse especially at night to meditate and pray. Sometimes, in his meditation, words would escape his mind and come to light. It was like he could hear them approach from the distance. The media power was employed as a tool to further this cause...

AUTHENTICATED. It's in the news
It does not matter your views
Whether you believe it or not
It is raining diamonds from heaven above

There's being a pole shift
The sun now rises in the west and set in the east
Whether you see it or not
Aliens have emerged from the earth's crust

The trumpet has sounded
People are being caught up in the skies
I know you are still in doubt like Thomas
Judgement day is right here before our very eyes

An apocalyptic plague is creeping in the air
Humans are being eaten by a virus scare
It is neither here nor there
Put on your masquerade and swallow your fears.

Nkemcho was gradually falling asleep but he desired to read on.

Zan Gusto tried everything he could to keep his people believing in him and standing strong behind his back. It was rather late because the country had been divided into two major ideologies. The rate of in-fighting within his cabinet and attack on the integrity of his administration weakened his grip on power.

This affected the economic activities and the gross domestic product adversely. The people began to murmur and complain when they could not enjoy life the way they had been used to in the past. Somewhere in the east, a rebel movement was born. It gathered momentum and in no time, they began to advance towards the capital city of Wakanabe. Zan Gusto was ready to fight till his last breath. He gathered his army and went to war with the rebel movement backed by the Super 8.

In the end, darkness returned to Motema. Zan Gusto was slaughtered in the street of Wakanabe amidst total devastation. One of the attacking rebel soldiers reached for the President's pocket to search for valuables but found a folded piece of paper. He opened it gently and it read thus: "You are the devil you fear…"

You are the devil you fear
You are the cross you bear
You are the failure you
dread
You are what you prepared

You are the love you crave

You are the fire ablaze
You are darkness in light days
You are the lost in a maze

In you is light and truth
With you lie wickedness of the fool
It's up to you to choose
A life of evil or good

You are the shadow you dread
Through you come the daily bread
No one else can sleep in your bed
Or break the chains holding your head

For you the universe revolves
And all the things thereof
Your soul no one can save
So, you be the only one to blame.

Nkemcho drifted off in deep slumber. The book in his hand fell and dropped on the soft brown rug. Tiredness had massacred his body so much that he started to snore heavily. The soul took off in a flight and wandered across the universe. A new life beyond opened up for him and he began to witness incredible things.

The earth woke up to a brand-new age. A century had just gone by and it carried with it all the things of old. The reality of the day was stranger than fiction. It was a wonder to behold but very scary for the faint-hearted. Although the weak in body and spirit had all been taken care of by process of holistic elimination, some people were still so scared of the heaven that was staring them in the face. The big cities were empty and very quiet. The air so clean as pollution had been totally eliminated. There were no longer machines and vehicles running on diesel or petrol. The use of extremely clean energy had come to stay. There were no cars on the streets and no conventional aircraft in the skies yet movement from one point to the other was proportionate to jet speed.

Flying vehicles had replaced all manner of urban transportation. It was a thing of the past to find a place where people were gathered as a group. It was more of individual kind of existence that was practiced. The new species of humans have gotten used to this and life just went on quite smoothly. The only exception were a few people who came from the past to the future. Emily from Quebec in Canada was one of them.

Emily wished her husband had joined her in the decision to have their bodies frozen for one hundred years after they had died. For her she did not enjoy the later part of her past life because she had cancer of the breasts which finally terminated her life on earth. In order not to lose at both ends, she decided to buy into the new technology that offered her another life in the distant future. A future where the cure for all forms of deadly diseases would have been discovered.

As she stepped out of the facility where her body had been kept for ten decades, she wondered how life in the new world would look like. She had been assured not to bother about anything because all her worries had been taken care of before she was awoken from the deep sleep. All questions, she was told, must be addressed to a device that has been installed in her home and connected to a micro-chip in her right palm.

Mobile phones have been outdated. Everyone wore a device like sunglasses that performed the task of communication in all its ramifications. The device it was that told them who was calling without a single ring. The device also had the capability of automatically correcting peoples' vision. All other operations were performed by voice command and thought patterns.

"I understand there are no more countries."

"That's right, Ma'am."

"No presidents…"

"Yes…" He chuckled.

"And no religion."

"That's correct, ma'am." She continued her walk with this strange man through a shiny lighted corridor. Every time they walked through a door, a beep sounded and lights of different colours danced back and forth. Emily wondered what all that meant. She was not in the mood for too many questions. She had been told that every enquiry had been taken care of. There was something about her companion. He appeared very clean, intelligent and conducted himself to perfection. Emily spied at him severally as they descended to a soft platform. He did not appear to her like a normal human being. At least not like the ones she used to know in her past world.

"I feel very much at peace but a little anxious."

"I know."

Emily was ferried in a tube-like structure to the roof top where a mini-sized flying object was waiting to convey her to her new abode. The male attendant gestured with a light wave at the vehicle and the doors opened. It was then that Emily realised that there was no one in the vehicle.

"I didn't realise that you're a pilot?" Emily smiled.

"There's no pilot, ma'am. It's programmed. It flies on artificial intelligence." He beckoned to her to step in. Then he entered, sat down comfortably, and fastened their seat belts. Then he touched a button. The doors closed and a voice from the cockpit began to issue out instructions. He responded simply by touching certain buttons as the voice directed. The propellers started to roll, and gained momentum and speed. The flying object effortlessly lifted off the ground and dashed into the city skyline. Emily took a wide view of the open sky. It was adorned with super structures. Her mind opened and she began to float in the ocean of creative impulse. She felt the power as it unleashed the first line. She heard the poetic rendition as it gathered momentum. Line after line, she saw all the things that the spirit was labouring to tell her.

The green jungle of sparkling tall green trees
Made from glass, iron, and plastic
Adorn the skyline glee

The air is sweet,
Like nectar from honeybees
But the cities in all its beauty appear empty

Where have all the people gone?
To hell and back is the song
That play all-night long

Strange things become ace
And bellow at your race
As the sunlight strikes you in the face

Flying objects
Like metal insects
Build up humanity nests

Acting like organised swarms of locusts in successive row
Strange things hit us in the belly below,
Not knowing where we'd go

They fold the weather in their pockets
The iron wings, eat up the rockets
Humanity caged in the sockets

Strange things pretending to be the best
Of fantasies laid to rest
Strange things under the seabed

Emily watched with great amazement as the object began to slow down. It began to glide as it approached a gigantic structure in green. They had been airborne for only five minutes but it seemed that they had covered several hundreds of kilometres. The portable craft hovered for a while and steadied in one position. The engine sound changed from a smooth roll into an almost noiseless flap. Gradually, it touched down the way it had taken off in this high-rise building. This gigantic structure that looked very much like a very tall tree had its entire walls covered in plants and beautiful flowers. The surrounding buildings were similar but varied in size and design. Emily actually felt like she was dreaming. It didn't appear real. The doors opened again and they stepped out. The doors closed gently, and this strange-looking man repeated the same ritual with a light wave. The engine came alive in a couple of seconds the flying taxi was lost in the sky.

"This is unbelievable, mister…"

"Jones. Gary Jones but you can call me Gary."

They stood on a square platform for a few seconds. Emily started to wonder how they would descend from the terrace. Gary smiled with the corner of his lips as he enjoyed the woman's perplexed demeanour. He had an idea of what was going on in her mind.

"Stand firm, ma'am. We're about to descend."

Emily looked at Gary surprisingly. She was just about to ask how that was going to be possible when the platform made a click-like sound and started to descend slowly into the building. The entire platform went down into the structure.

"You're on the five-hundred and fifth floor, ma'am."

"You're kidding me."

"The building has six hundred floors."

"That's incredible."

Gary smiled and looked away.

Emily's apartment was nothing like she had imagined. It was all empty. She gave a frowning look at Gary expecting an explanation. Gary walked straight to the window and observed the skyline. She felt a bit uneasy and wondered why he ignored her concerns. Emily waited to see if he would come up with an explanation. Gary turned around and walked close to where Emily was standing. It was clear that she was terribly disappointed.

"This is all yours now. Like I said, any questions should be addressed to *Genie*. It knows all the answers to our questions."

"Genie?"

"Yes, Genie." She sighed.

"What type of apartment is this? No television, no bed… nothing… How will I survive? It's an empty house?"

Gary smiled.

"It's not an empty house. I said you can ask *Genie* any question whatsoever."

"No, you're kidding me."

"Every gadget in the house responds to your voice."

"How?"

"Do you feel like sitting down for instance?"

"Hell, yes…"

"Then call for your sofa… or simply ask *Genie* to activate your sofa."

"Oh, I see."

"Every other thing in the house works that way."

"This is amazing."

"You can test that now, ma'am."

Emily sighed and cleared her throat.

"*Genie*, I want to sit down." A voice appeared from nowhere and asked what type of chair that she wanted. Then the voice gave the various options available. Emily thought this was incredible.

"Sofa, please." A click followed and a shift in the wall unfolded a cream-coloured sofa. Emily looked at Gary.

"It worked. Thanks, Gary." Gary nodded.

"My pleasure, ma'am. Like I said earlier on, you can call for anything with your voice command. Every house in the country is structured in like manner. If the option of your choice is not available, *genie* will let you know and propose an alternative. I will take my leave now. Once again, welcome to the new world."

"Thank you, Gary."

Gary took his leave and Emily just wandered around the apartment experimenting with technology. It was quite unbelievable. As she moved around and discovered more incredible things, the creative force found her again. This time, she was not imagining anything. Her voice was loud and clear. She sang these words. The melody was so nice. It was also very emotional. The canary, songbird of the Macaronesia Islands would have been very jealous.

Beautiful like a newly born, I sniff the pain of joy
Beckoning to me
This is new, my new world, painting pictures
Of strange realities

We had it all
Affection that was hot like hell
I gave my wall all up, cos
He had struck me with a deadly spell

Same me, only budded thrice
Then the wall cracked and crumbled
I became a non-desirable
In my face I stood miserable

Sexy did no longer work the magic
Like my French lingerie did
Nature's engine house started to rust
So, my desires remained unfulfilled

But I took an oath
Wasn't going to give myself to another

I became a man and a woman
The only way to avoid the crater

A fellow prisoner it was
Who sold me technology?
I'm now an addict
But I still desire my nemesis

***

The phone rang several times before Nkemcho struggled out of bed. He picked it up and looked at the call history.

"God!"

He rushed into the bathroom, brushed his teeth and had a quick shower. Then he jumped into a white caftan and rushed out of the house. The meeting with the governor was billed to start in an hour. The next weekend had been programmed for a trip to the village. His schedule was tight. The elders of Owu had waded into the dispute between him and Amara. It was a thing of tradition to intervene in matters like that with a bid to finding some kind of solution to it. Amara had returned to the village much earlier but Nkemcho was a city man. The memories of the past haunted him day and night. He had also made up his mind never to take Amara back. In fact, if it was not for the respect he had for the elders, he would have rejected any offer for a discussion on his marital crisis.

The village setting remained the same; the people, the houses, the roads and bush paths. Everything was in its usual place. All evidence of accelerated development had suddenly come to a halt. It simply showed how much the sons and daughters of Owu land who had migrated to the city in search of greener pastures, fared at that moment in time. The elders gathered in a semi-circle arrangement. The centre was bare. To the left beside a tree was a black goat. There was a keg of red palm oil and a big wrap of kola nuts. Behind the benches to the right-hand side were about five ten litre jerrycans, made of plastic, filled with fresh palm wine. The meeting was set. Nkemcho and his family members sat to the right while Amara and her people sat to the left. Elder Ukulekulu, who was the oldest man in the clan declared the meeting open with a long prayer. He did not mince words as he told them the reason why everybody was gathered at that venue which was usually used for relaxation after a hard days' work.

"We all know the reason why we are here." Everybody nodded in different styles and fashion. Amara's face never left the ground. The gravity of her offence was too much to stand the privy eyes of her in-laws. Nkemcho, on the other hand, maintained a calm comportment. He had fought hard to overcome the adverse effects of such a huge betrayal.

"Our father. You've spoken well. We all appreciate your effort in making sure that this meeting is taking place today. You will last a long time in power for us." Elder Kiyeku, who represented Nkemcho's father concluded. The convener of the meeting, elder Ukulekulu acknowledged the compliment. Then he cleared his cracked throat once again. He always did that before he spoke.

"After an extensive and rigorous investigation that involved the chief priest and priestess of the entire Owuland, we were able to come up with the details of what took place. Nkemcho and Amara are both our children. So, whatever affects them, at the same time affects us. Whatever happened between them was not entirely their fault, the findings concluded. We are traditional people and we have laws of our ancestors that remain binding on us. We also know that there are severe consequences for anyone who breaks any of these laws."

"That's very correct," agreed everyone almost at the same time.

"The gods were very angry because an abominable act had been committed. I need recall that both Nkemcho's parents were murdered by Ikwere people during the last crisis that we had with them. We did not understand the reason for that cruel act until now."

"Elder, go straight to the point. We're not going to sleep here." The leader of Amara's family, Elder Baruka cut in. It sounded quite rude but no one seemed to pay attention to the distraction as they all focussed on the old man who was running the show.

"Nkemcho's parents were killed because the gods sought revenge for what the man did. I mean Nkemcho's father."

This statement sent a series of queries into the facial expression of everyone there. Then the old man dropped his head for a few seconds and shook it sadly.

"We are all ears, elder," said Elder Baruka whose patience was fast running out.

"Amara's mother and Nkemcho's father were lovers."

It was a bombshell. Amara's mother dropped her head into her lap. Her husband turned to her in utter shock.

"So, you were sleeping with him?" The anger in the man's voice was loaded with bile.

"We're not here to fight but to heal our wounds. The gods demand that the truth be told to take away the reproach and indignation." The old man continued. "Amara and Nkemcho fell in love and got married. It was not supposed to be. That was the reason why they could not produce offspring of their type. However, Amara got entangled with another man and had children of him. It was the revelation of that affair, which was made possible through the white man's technology, that led to the events that finally brought us together in this place. Amara and Nkemcho could not have children together because it's an abomination to mix the same bloodline."

"Abomination?" Nkemcho asked. He looked dazed.

"Yes! Abomination." The look in the old man's face changed to that of one who was utterly disappointed. "The affair between Nkemcho's father and Amara's mother produced an issue. That child is this woman here — Amara. Amara and Nkemcho have the same father. They are brother and sister." The entire meeting place erupted. Nkemcho jumped out of his seat. Amara tumbled on the floor and began to roll in the sand. Her mother simply put both her hands on her head and cried.

"Unbelievable!" Nkemcho kept repeating the word.

"Please, let's maintain decorum. It's a bad thing but we must honour the gods by this confession and then we can go on with the purification and cleansing." Another elder who had not spoken all this while chipped in, trying to control the emotions that had taken control of the entire arena.

"Thank you, Elder Shukuka." The old man took charge once more. "We have not come here to play the blame game. Humans are not perfect, so they make mistakes. The only problem is that some of these mistakes do have very serious consequences. We are here for peace and continuity. Therefore, I command the cleansing to begin after which we will all re-converge here and make merry. Oman, Ikedy, Mama

Edna, Sister Huju. Please take Amara and her mother to the riverside for the purification and cleansing. The rest of us will wait here for them to finish and come back to us."

The people that he mentioned sprang to their feet and led the two women down the road towards the river, while the rest discussed in low tones. They took with them, the black goat, the keg of red palm oil and a jerrycan of palm wine. The goat was to be sacrificed to appease the gods while the palm wine was to be used to bath the women and their entire body polished with the red palm oil at the end of the purification exercise. Nkemcho stared at the two women as they were led out of the venue. He kept repeating the word 'unbelievable' and rubbed his palms together. His mind raced back to the storytelling session where his mom had told the story of the Owuan people. The words of Okotoba echoed into his ears. His body started to catch some strange chill. Then he closed his eyes, his mouth opened up slowly and the words began to drop. It was a simple question.

"And who are these gods?" He repeated the question and switched off from the gathering.

***

The native doctor left them as they stared helplessly at their son. Nkemcho's father sat close to the boy and veered into empty space, not wanting to express his disappointment. His wife, on the other hand, lay beside her motionless son in total anguish, but hoping that the gods who watched over the affairs of men would have mercy upon her. An hour had passed. The deadline period had elapsed. Nkemcho's father walked across the room, his hands crossed at his back. The worst had happened. He felt terrible at the sight of his son and his mother as she cried.

"Forgive me, fathers. Your love for us never fades. We remain your children and your protection upon us is eternal. Your decision I cannot change but I know you judge well." He had not finished the last statement when the atmosphere unfolded a dramatic turn. Then the miraculous happened. The boy sneezed, and tried to move his head from side to side. The woman and her husband jumped around almost at the same time and knelt before the boy.

"Did you hear that?" asked the husband.

"The gods are not asleep," she sang repeatedly.

Then they helped him up to a sitting position; and supported him from both sides. His eyes opened. It was a great relief. They could not believe their eyes. The unfolding situation felt like the arrival of a newly born baby.

"Go boil some water quickly." The woman dashed out of the scene at lightning speed. After his wife had left, he went behind and sat at the boy's back and continued to assure him that all was well. After about twenty minutes, Nkemcho's mother arrived with a kettle filled with warm water and they administered some to him. He sipped the water slowly from a plastic cup for five to ten minutes before he found his voice.

"What happened?" he asked his parents.

"You need some rest. You were a bit ill," said his father. Then he looked at the mother as if to ask for permission to narrate the ordeal.

"Let him rest first." The mother was still very afraid.

"I'm okay, Mother. I've been listening to you tell us stories. You told a lot of stories and I remember all of them like my name." His words were very coherent.

"Yes…"

"Mother, you told us the story of the Owuan people and many other stories like that of the great musician from overseas and that of the Great King I Am, and so many others. And there was this story of a young man who got married to his sister unknowingly and they couldn't have kids. His name coincidentally was Nkemcho… there was a lot more. And that of the future world where today the life we know kind of expired and gave way to a far advanced civilisation." Nkemcho's mother turned slightly to his father.

"What is he talking about? Are you sure he's all right?"

"He must still be drowsy. It will be well, my dear."

Nkemcho looked around again, to his father and then to his mother. He noticed the confusion in their faces but could not understand why. However, he worried less about this because he felt very secure to have had his parents around him at that time. It gave him a great delight. Then he sighed.

"It took a long time before we could get through the entire stories but I particularly enjoyed every bit of it. It was as if I was present in all the action that took place. It was awesome. Where are the other kids?"

"They just left."

It was not an option now to inform the boy that he had been unconscious for fourteen solid days.

"It was like some long journey, mother. I'm totally exhausted"

"I'm grateful to the gods that you came back. I was so scared." His mother finally spilled the beans. She could not take her eyes off him.

"Came back? From where?" Nkemcho stared at his mother, a bit confused.

Then Father waded in to control the conversation.

"Woman, the gods have done well. Let's celebrate the goodness of our ancestors. Give the boy some food, I beg of you. I will quickly hurry to the elders place to give them the good news."

In no time, normalcy returned to Nkemcho. His speech resumed unhindered. He started to walk around the compound although he felt very weak for lack of energy. He had been without food and water for fourteen days. The joy that soon returned to his mother's heart was unspeakable. His father had allowed faith to prevail over hopelessness. It was a great day in the sense that it marked the victory of life over death. The uninvited guest almost had its way if not for the timely intervention of the gods.

And everything he saw came to pass.